SCARIEST. BOOK. EVER.

R.L. STINE

SCHOLASTIC INC.

Goosebumps book series created by Parachute Press, Inc.

ISBN 978-1-339-01498-2

10 9 8 7 6 5 4 3 2 1 23 24 25 26 27

Printed in the U.S.A. 40
First printing 2023

PART ONE

1

"PLEASE DON'T LEAVE US!"

Uncle Wendell loved to make up strange and frightening stories. So when he told my sister Betty and me about the scariest book ever written, we didn't believe him.

We knew he was trying to scare us. We were onto him. We only pretended to shiver and shudder.

Of course, we *should* have believed him about the Scariest Book Ever.

Because that story about the book was true.

The truth is, Betty and I didn't want to stay with Uncle Wendell. As we made the long drive to his house, even Bellamy, our dog, was barking unhappily in the back-seat beside us.

Bellamy is a five-year-old shepherd-terrier mix, and he's usually an angel in the car. But he knew something was up. He knew we were heading somewhere new and strange. So he didn't stop yapping.

We had been driving for hours. Trees whirred by in a green blur outside the car window. We were racing past some kind of forest.

"Mom, listen," I said. I leaned forward in my seat behind her and tapped her shoulder.

"Stop tapping me, Billy," she said. "You're like a woodpecker. You've been tapping me the whole drive."

"That's because I'm trying to get through to you," I said.

"You two have made your point," Dad growled, hunched over the steering wheel. "But you don't have a point. The only point is on the tops of your heads!"

Dad was a stand-up comic before he went into real estate. And he still thinks he's funny.

"We know you're anxious about staying with your uncle Wendell," Mom said.

"Anxious?" Betty cried. "We're not anxious. We don't want to stay with a total stranger for two weeks."

"Not so loud," Dad muttered.

"I can't help it. I was born with a loud voice," Betty replied. Betty is tough. She never lets Dad have the last word. And she never pretends to laugh at his jokes like I do.

My sister and I are twins. Billy and Betty, the Arnold

twins. Dad always tells people we're identical twins. And that doesn't even begin to be funny. We don't even look alike. She's tall and thin and I'm at least four inches shorter.

Twins are supposed to be close to one another, and we get along okay. Of course, everything isn't perfect. Mom told Betty she was ten minutes older than me. So she thinks she's the boss. The big sister.

I don't know why Mom had to tell her that. If I was ten minutes older, I wouldn't make such a big deal about it.

I was still leaning over Mom. The car hit a bump in the road, and it sent me sailing back into my seat.

Dad laughed. "This is a thrill ride," he said, watching me in the rearview mirror.

I growled. "You know I hate roller coasters."

"Everybody, simmer down," Mom said.

"Billy and I are simmered *up*," Betty said. "You said Uncle Wendell is a weird one. I heard you saying that to Dad. So why are we staying with him?"

"He was the only person who could take you both for two weeks," Mom said. "We have no other family. We've been over this, haven't we?"

“You two are *both* weird ones,” Dad said, a grin on his face. “So you’ll get along fine.”

Betty rubbed Bellamy’s belly, and he rolled onto his back and stopped yapping for a while. Betty is his favorite. When I rub his belly, he tries to bite me.

I had to sneeze. I tried to hold it in. But a loud blast escaped my nose and mouth.

“Billy, cover your nose,” Dad said.

“There wasn’t time,” I told him. “You know I always sneeze when I’m tense or upset.”

“Think you could try to outgrow that habit?” Dad asked.

“Why can’t we go to London with you?” I demanded for the hundredth time.

Dad groaned. “I told you, Billy. It’s a business trip. Not a family vacation.”

“The two weeks will fly by,” Mom said. She turned in her seat. “Can I just talk seriously to you for two minutes?”

“Okay. We’ll grant you permission,” Betty replied. Sometimes she acts like she’s a queen or something.

“I know you have no memory of Wendell,” Mom said. “He saw you when you were babies. But I think you’re really going to like him. He—”

"You said he was weird," I said, "and his house sits all by itself in a forest with no one around for miles."

"You are going to *love* his old house," Dad chimed in. "And it isn't just *any* forest. It's called the Wayward Forest."

Betty rolled her eyes. "Huh? Wayward? Why do they call it that?"

"Beats me," Dad said. He swerved to miss a hole in the road.

"You didn't let me finish," Mom said, reaching for a water bottle. "You two like to read. You're both bookworms."

"Ugh," Betty groaned. "Why do we have to be worms?"

"Well, Wendell has an amazing collection of books," Mom said. "I think you will go nuts when you explore his library."

"Yeah. Nuts," I repeated sarcastically.

"And his house is filled with wild gadgets and strange objects he has found all over the world," Mom added. "The house is like a museum."

"Awesome. I always wanted to live in a museum," I muttered.

Dad slapped his hand on the steering wheel. "Bad

attitude!" he shouted. "Both of you. Bad attitude! You should be open to new experiences."

"I don't want experiences," I said. "I just want to stay with someone I know."

"I'll bet when we come to pick you up in two weeks, you won't want to leave," Mom said.

It was my turn to roll my eyes. I wanted to say: *"How much do you want to bet?"*

But I didn't say it.

An hour later, Dad gripped the steering wheel tightly in both hands. He gritted his teeth. "I think we're totally lost. Mom and I are going to miss our flight," he said.

Mom patted his arm. "We'll be okay. I'm sure we're close to Wendell's house."

We had swung off the highway. The dirt roads through the forest twisted and curved through the trees, and Dad got turned around twice.

"We're making a circle," he said. "I remember that pile of rocks."

"Go straight. Go straight." Mom pointed out the windshield. "I think we're okay."

Dad shook his head. "I—I was counting on the navigation system to get us there."

The GPS had gone out as soon as we turned off the highway.

"Yaaay!" I cried. "Does this mean we get to go to London with you?"

"Be quiet, Billy!" Dad shouted. "You're not helpful at all."

I sank back in my seat. Betty stared out the window. "We can't be lost," she said. "People don't get lost any-more, do they?"

"No. We're not," Mom said. "Look! I think that's Wendell's house. I see it back in the trees."

Dad mopped the sweat off his forehead with one hand. "Whew. Lucky the house is so tall. Whoa. Look at it. Rising high above the treetops."

The car bumped into a small clearing. Dad turned into a long, pebbly driveway that led past a grassy front lawn up to the house.

Now I could see the house clearly. It wasn't shaped like a house. It rose straight up like a tower. A solid black tower. The afternoon sunlight didn't reflect off it. It made me think of blackboard slate.

I could see a narrow door. A row of tiny windows along the front of the house.

"Is it a house or a fort?" Betty asked.

Mom and Dad didn't answer. They were already

standing in the driveway, pulling our suitcases from the trunk.

Bellamy scratched his paws against the window. It had been a long drive for the poor guy. I could see he was desperate to get out.

I grabbed his leash, pushed open the door, and slid my feet to the ground. Bellamy wagged his tail happily and tried to tug me toward the woods.

The sun hung low over the forest, and the air felt cool and fresh. Birds trilled and whooped, as if greeting us.

Dad checked the time on his phone. "Whoa. We are so late. We really have to hurry."

He carried our suitcases to the front door and dropped them. He pushed the brass doorbell.

Betty and I hung back, waiting for Uncle Wendell to appear. What did he look like? I had no memory of him.

With an impatient sigh, Dad pushed the doorbell again.

Silence.

No Uncle Wendell.

Dad pounded his fist on the door.

"I'll bet he went into town to buy groceries," Mom said. "He asked for a list of all the food you two like."

Dad shook his head. "We can't wait here. We'll miss

our flight." He mopped sweat off his forehead. "I'm so sorry, but we have to go. Everything will be fine. I'm sure Wendell will be back any minute."

He grabbed Mom's arm and started to pull her to the car.

"You're just going to leave us here?" I called after them.

"Apologize to Wendell for us," Mom said. "Tell him we didn't want to miss our plane."

She bent to pet the dog. "Take good care of Bellamy," she said. "And have fun. Text us as soon as Wendell arrives so we know you're okay."

They climbed into the car and closed the doors. We watched them back down the driveway and roar away, the pebbles flying from under the tires.

I opened my mouth in a loud sneeze. You can guess I was a little tense.

I wiped my nose with my sleeve and pushed the doorbell again.

No answer.

Suddenly, Bellamy began tugging us away from the door, pulling hard on his leash. The dog opened his jaws and began to howl.

Betty and I gazed up at the strange black house. The late afternoon sunlight glinted off its tiny windows.

Bellamy howled louder.

"What's wrong with him?" Betty asked. "Does he know something we don't know?"

"IS THIS THE WRONG HOUSE?"

"Bellamy, what's your problem?" I demanded. "Stop howling."

He dug his paws into the ground and refused to budge. Finally, Betty bent down and petted his back, soothing him.

"I think he picked up on our fear," I said. I'd read a thing online about how dogs can sense how their owners feel.

"I'm not afraid," Betty said, shaking her head. "I just don't want to do this. Where is Uncle Wendell? Is he home or not?"

I thought maybe Bellamy's howls would bring Wendell outside. But the door remained closed. Silence inside.

We both stared at the narrow black door. Bellamy had stopped howling. But his back was still tensed.

I pounded my fist on the door. It didn't make much of a sound. The door seemed very thick.

Betty shivered. The air had grown chilly in the shadow of the house. A breeze had started to pick up, and the trees all shook and whispered. A big brown rabbit stood on its hind legs and stared at us from the tall grass of the front lawn.

We gazed at each other, waiting for Wendell to open the door.

Waiting.

"Maybe Mom was right. Maybe he went out," I said. My voice trembled a little.

"But he's expecting us," Betty said, staring at the door. "He knows we're arriving this afternoon." She shivered again. Bellamy shivered, too.

I closed my fist and pounded some more, this time, as hard as I could.

A bird cawed loudly from somewhere behind us.

Now I shivered. Was it trying to warn us away?

I turned and walked to the tiny window nearest the door. Shielding my eyes with both hands, I peered into the house.

Total darkness.

"No lights on," I told Betty. "I can't see anything."

"He *has* to be in there," Betty said, rubbing Bellamy's back. She opened her mouth and began to shout. "Uncle Wendell? Wendell! We're out here. Can you hear us?"

Silence.

The brown rabbit turned and scampered into the trees.

"Wendell? Wendell? Are you there?" Betty tried again.

I stepped up to the door. I raised my fist to pound on it one more time. But then I had a better idea.

I wrapped my hand around the small brass door knob. I turned it and pushed. And the door creaked open.

Bellamy made a *yip* sound and tried to back away.

I pushed the door open farther. Betty grabbed Bellamy and pulled him inside with us.

It was almost as dark as night. We both stopped and waited for our eyes to adjust. The air felt cold and damp, and the room smelled musty, as if it hadn't been dusted in a very long time.

I rubbed my hand over the wall, and it bumped a light switch. A gray light washed down from the ceiling high above us.

Blinking, I peered around the room. It was a huge

square room with a ceiling a mile high. I saw a long wooden table with two chairs behind it. And there were two overstuffed lounge chairs at the far end of the room.

Bellamy took off for one of the overstuffed chairs. "Come back!" Betty called. Her voice echoed off the walls. But the dog ignored her. He was too busy sniffing it.

I cupped my hands around my mouth. "Wendell!" I shouted. "Hey, Uncle Wendell. It's Billy and Betty. We're here!"

The words echoed into the distance.

I heard a *creak*. I thought maybe Wendell was finally coming. But no. It must have been old house noises.

"Wendell? Wendell?" Betty and I both called his name.

Still no answer.

I turned to my sister. "Didn't Mom say his house was filled with books and all kinds of crazy objects?"

She nodded.

"Well, look around," I said. "No books anywhere. The room is nearly bare. No weird objects and not a single book."

Betty wrinkled her forehead. She took a deep, shuddering breath. "Do you think maybe this is the wrong house?"

A TRAP

We called Wendell's name some more. Our voices echoed as if we were in a cave.

I spotted a door at the other end of the room. It was open. Nothing but darkness behind it.

"Wendell! Uncle Wendell? Are you here?"

We really didn't expect an answer, so we both jumped when a man came rumbling through the doorway.

He took four or five heavy steps, boots thudding loudly on the floor. Then he stopped and his eyes went wide when he saw us.

Startled, Betty and I froze. Bellamy barked once, then stood at attention.

He was a big man with a lion's mane of black hair, wild around his head, and a spiky black beard. He wore a loose-fitting, plaid lumberjack shirt over baggy khaki pants and black knee-high boots.

He squinted at us, his big chest heaving up and down,

breathless, as if he didn't expect us. He rubbed his beard with a pudgy hand. "Hello there," he said finally. His voice was deep and scratchy.

"Uncle Wendell?" I said. "We—"

"You're here," he said. His black eyes studied us. They moved from Betty to me. He rubbed his beard some more, as if he was thinking hard.

"Our parents were late," Betty said. "They couldn't stay to see you. They are sorry, but—"

"You've grown," he said in his rumbly voice.

"Betty and I are twelve," I said.

He nodded. Then he took a few steps closer. "I want to apologize. I was out back. I wasn't here to greet you."

"That's okay," I said. "We—we're so glad—"

Wendell lowered his eyes. "I'm afraid you've come at a bad time."

"A bad time?"

What did he mean by *that*?

"But can we still stay here?" Betty asked.

"Yes. You *must* stay here," he said. "I need your help."

He waved a big hand, motioning for us to follow him.

Betty and I exchanged glances. *What is going on here? Why does he need our help?*

He led us down a dark hall to a room near the back of the house. Bellamy followed, bumping us from behind as we walked. The dog didn't want us out of his sight.

The room was huge. A fire flamed in a wide stone fireplace that nearly took up the whole wall. A black couch and two black armchairs circled a low coffee table.

The table was stacked high with books. Piles of books were stacked against one wall.

Guess we're in the right house after all, I thought.

Wendell motioned for Betty and me to sit down on the couch. He dropped heavily into one of the armchairs. Bellamy tried to climb on Betty's lap. He's always trying to do that, but he's too big. He finally settled on the floor next to her feet.

A groan escaped Wendell's lips. "Something terrible has happened," he said. "I can't believe it. The book . . ." His voice trailed off.

"Book? What book?" I asked.

"We have to get it back," he said. He was staring over our heads. I realized he wasn't talking to us. He was talking to himself. "Have to get the book back . . ."

"A book is missing?" Betty asked.

He lowered his eyes to us. It was as if he suddenly remembered we were there.

"The book . . . it was stolen," he said in a whisper.

"A valuable book?" I asked.

"It's a long story," he answered. "I'll tell you all about it later. Let's get you settled into your rooms. Then we can talk."

We both stared at him. *A book was stolen? Why is he being so mysterious about it? Does he always act this weird?*

"Sorry your timing is so bad," he murmured. "But we'll make the most of it." He spread his hands over the arms of the chair and pushed himself to his feet. "Let me show you to your rooms."

Betty and I stood up. Bellamy jumped to his feet, too.

Wendell frowned at the dog. "I'm really sorry about this," he said. "But there are many valuables in the house. Your dog must stay outside."

"No!" I cried. "Bellamy doesn't wreck things. And he's used to being inside with us."

"I'm sorry," Wendell said, still frowning at the dog. "We'll take good care of him. I promise."

Betty hugged the dog's neck. "No. Please. Give Bellamy a chance."

"Wish I could," Wendell said. He turned and shouted down the long hallway. "Jesse—come take the dog to the back lawn."

A few seconds later, a young woman in a pale blue sweater pulled down over black tights appeared. She stared at Betty and me as if she was shocked to see us.

"This is Jesse," Wendell said. "She'll see that your dog is safe and happy." He turned to her. "You haven't met Billy and Betty. But they are your cousins."

"Nice to meet you," Jesse said.

"You're Wendell's daughter?" I said.

She nodded.

Weird, I thought. *Why didn't Mom and Dad mention that Wendell has a daughter?*

Jesse reached for Bellamy.

Betty pulled him back. "Do we have to?"

"Afraid so," Wendell said softly. "I have so many valuables to protect." He sighed. "And the most valuable thing of them all has been stolen. We'll be too busy searching for it. We won't have time to worry about the dog."

Betty hesitated for a long moment. Then she let Jesse lead the dog away.

"He's real cute," Jesse said. "You can come visit him out back all you want." Her shoes clicking on the floor, she disappeared down the hall with him.

"Follow me. Your rooms are upstairs," Wendell said.

He led us down the hall to a steep wooden stairway. "Hold on to the banister," he said. "This house is old, and some of the stairs are weak."

The stairs creaked and groaned under our feet as we climbed. Upstairs, a row of rooms opened to our right. The wall on our left was lined with bookshelves.

"I think you'll be comfortable—" Wendell started.

But a loud *SNAP* interrupted him.

I cried out in surprise. And then a stab of hot pain roared up my ankle. Howling like a wild animal, I dropped to the floor.

4

A DANCING BEAR

A light flashed on overhead. Sprawled on my back, I stared up at it, screaming.

"Oh noooo." I heard Uncle Wendell murmur over my moans. He dropped beside me and reached for my leg.

I raised my head and saw what was causing the throbbing pain. A trap. A very large mousetrap. Clamped over my ankle.

My leg felt on fire. The pain roared up my whole body.

I glimpsed Betty backed against the wall with her hands over her face.

Wendell leaned over me, pulling the trap apart with both hands. Finally, he snapped it open. I kicked my leg free and rolled onto my side.

Wendell tossed the big mousetrap aside and bent to massage my ankle. "The skin isn't broken," he said. "The pain will fade, Billy. Take a few deep breaths."

He rubbed the ankle, and the pain did seem to lessen. After a few minutes, he helped me to my feet. “Okay. Try to walk. Lean against the wall if you have to,” he said.

He kept a hand on my shoulder as I took a few steps. “I—I’m okay,” I stammered. My leg worked fine. The pain had faded to a dull ache.

Wendell stayed by my side, shaking his head. “I’m so sorry, Billy,” he said. “I thought I picked up all the traps.”

“Wendell, why was there a big trap in the hall?” Betty called from behind us.

“I set them there to stop any thieves.” He sighed. “Too bad the thief got away. And the only person I caught in a trap was Billy.”

He stopped and pointed. “This door leads to your rooms.”

Betty and I turned into the doorway—and we both let out startled cries.

A bear. A giant black bear—at least ten feet tall—stared down at us in the doorway. Jaws open, teeth bared, its enormous paws raised to attack.

I jumped back. Bumped into Betty. And we both toppled into the wall.

Wendell laughed. “Meet Gus.”

“Gus?” Betty and I both said at once.

He patted the bear's big belly. "He's stuffed. Gus was embalmed eighty years ago. He doesn't look his age, does he?"

I started to breathe normally. "There are too many surprises here," I muttered.

"He's a dancing bear," Wendell said. "I taught him to dance."

We both blinked. "But you said—" I started.

Wendell nodded. "I said he died eighty years ago. But he lived behind this house in the Wayward Forest. The rules are different there." He smoothed the bear's belly fur.

Betty and I stared up at the bear's big head. The black eyes glowed as if the creature was alive.

"Once a year," Wendell said, "Gus comes alive during the blue harvest moon." He smiled at us. "It's next week. Maybe Gus will dance for you."

Betty laughed. "Mom said you like to make up stories."

Wendell squinted at us. "Stories?"

"You're joking about Gus—right?" I said.

"Sorry. I don't make jokes," Wendell answered. "I don't have a sense of humor."

I studied his face. He wasn't kidding. "So . . . you're saying this stuffed bear comes to life once a year?"

Wendell nodded. "I'll tell you all about the Wayward Forest," he said. "But let's get you unpacked first. Jesse brought your bags to your rooms. Get settled quickly. Then come downstairs."

He looked around and lowered his voice to a whisper. "Please hurry. Until the book is returned—we're not safe here."

Betty and I exchanged glances. Then we scooted past the giant stuffed bear and started to our rooms.

Betty stopped at the door to her room and turned to me. She had a troubled look on her face. "I know Mom and Dad said Uncle Wendell was weird," she whispered. "But do you think they knew *how* weird?" She frowned. "How could they leave us here . . . ?"

“WE’RE ALL IN GREAT DANGER”

A short while later, we found Uncle Wendell waiting for us at the end of a long wooden table in the center of the kitchen. He sat with his elbows on the table, stroking his black beard. His eyes were closed. He seemed to be deep in thought.

I gazed around the kitchen. There were no windows. A large fluorescent light hanging from the high ceiling cast an eerie blue glow on the floor. Dark, scratched wood cabinets covered three walls. The other wall held a tall bookshelf that reached the ceiling. The stove and refrigerator were black and looked old-fashioned, like from an old movie or something.

It wasn’t the bright modern kitchen you see in commercials.

Jesse turned from a gray tiled counter and carried snack plates to the table for Betty and me. Wendell finally opened his eyes and acted startled, as if he wasn’t expecting us.

He motioned for Betty and me to sit down across the table from him.

"Enjoy your sandwiches," Jesse said without looking at us. She spun away and walked out of the room.

Wendell raised a tall coffee mug to his mouth and took a long drink.

I suddenly realized I was hungry. All I'd eaten today was a bag of chips in the car.

I took a bite of the sandwich on my plate. It was some kind of meat on black bread. Betty stared across the table at me. She was chewing hard.

"What kind of meat is this?" I asked Wendell.

He shrugged and didn't answer.

I took another big bite. It wasn't bad. Just very chewy.

Wendell spun the coffee mug between his hands. "I have a lot to explain to you," he said. "Did your parents tell you about the Wayward Forest?"

"Not really," I said.

He rubbed his beard. "It's a private forest," he said. "The land belongs to my family. No one else has been allowed inside it for hundreds of years. And most of my family have never entered it, either. They were too frightened."

He took another long sip of coffee. I chewed a big chunk of my sandwich. I was starting to like it.

"The forest has been untouched by humans for many, many years," Wendell continued. "It has grown differently than any other forest."

"What do you mean?" I asked. "You mean the trees are different? The plants?"

He shook his head. "It's the creatures who inhabit the Wayward Forest that are different, Billy. They can't be found anywhere else."

I squinted at him, trying to understand. "You mean because no one has gone there?"

"I don't know why the forest animals are so unusual," he said. "Maybe because for hundreds of years no one has hunted them. No one has bothered them. No scientists have taken them out to study. No one has fed them or photographed them."

Betty put down her sandwich. "Are they dangerous?" she asked.

"Yes. Some of them are dangerous," Wendell said, "because they've had no contact with humans." He tapped the side of his mug with his index finger. His eyes darted from Betty to me.

"There are birds that date back to prehistoric times," he continued. "They've been allowed to grow free. I've seen robins and crows the size of raccoons."

"Whoa!" I exclaimed.

"I've seen worms as big as *you* rise up from the ground," Wendell said. "I've seen squirrels as big as dogs. They travel in packs and hunt rabbits."

I tried to picture the creatures he was describing. Mom had told us that Wendell loved to make up wild stories. So I knew these creatures weren't real.

Betty's eyes were wide. *You've got to be kidding me. I think she believes him*, I thought.

"There are packs of six-legged creatures," Wendell said. "I don't know what to call them. They scrabble over the ground like crabs and they bark like dogs."

That one made me laugh.

Wendell slammed his coffee mug on the table. "Don't laugh, Billy. These creatures aren't funny. They're dangerous. They are used to being in control. They don't like strangers."

"Uh . . . sorry," I muttered.

He leaned over the table, bringing his face close to mine. "When we enter the forest tomorrow to search for the thief who stole the book," he said in a low whisper,

"I must insist that we stay together. Keep close. Don't wander off on your own."

"We're going into the forest?" Betty asked. Her eyes opened wider than I'd ever seen.

"Yes, I'm afraid we must," Wendell answered.

"Tell us about the book," I demanded.

Wendell leaned even closer. "I can only tell you one thing," he whispered. "While the book is missing, we are all in great danger."

SCARIEST. BOOK. EVER.

"Follow me," Wendell said.

His chair scraped the floor as he climbed to his feet.

I took one last chewy bite of the meat sandwich. Betty and I followed him through a narrow door at the back of the kitchen.

A stone stairway at the end of the hall led to the basement. The air grew cooler as we followed Wendell down.

He flipped a switch and a ceiling light flashed on. Betty and I blinked, waiting for our eyes to adjust.

The basement was wide, with bookcases on all four walls. The shelves were filled with books. And books were piled in tall stacks all over the floor.

"How many books do you have?" I asked. My voice echoed off the basement walls.

Wendell shrugged. "I lost count years ago. I have thousands. This basement is just one of the rooms where I keep them."

He led us to a row of folding chairs facing the middle of the room. He pulled one out, spun it around, and sat down. Then he motioned for us to sit across from him.

He rubbed his beard and closed his eyes for a moment, thinking hard again.

The room was dusty. I fought back a sneeze. There were so many books . . . I felt like I was in a dream. I wanted to go to a shelf and read the titles. But I sat still, waiting for Uncle Wendell to speak.

"Uncle Wendell, why did you bring us down here?" I asked.

He kept his eyes shut. He didn't answer.

"Did you want to show us something down here?" Betty asked.

No answer.

I gasped when I saw the chains on the wall. They hung in the middle of a space between two of the bookcases. Thick chains attached to the wall with metal cuffs on the end. Two sets of them hung down to the floor.

I instantly thought of a movie I saw where prisoners were chained to a wall for days.

A cold chill ran down my back. I tapped Betty and pointed to the chains.

Her mouth dropped open, but she didn't make a sound.

"Wendell—those chains—" I started. "Why—?"

He finally opened his eyes. It was as if I woke him up.

"I'm going to tell you something and you're not going to believe it. But I swear I'm not making this up," he began. "I wish I were." His gaze went from Betty to me. "I brought you down here to show you where we'll lock up the thief when we catch him."

I swallowed. Betty and I stared hard at the chains on the wall.

He rubbed his beard. "Let me say this as plain as I can. The book that was stolen is the scariest book in the world."

He watched us, waiting for us to react. But I didn't move. I didn't know how to react to that.

Scariest book in the world? Huh?

Wendell sighed. "Of course, I had it locked up," he said. "Locked up tight, I thought." He sighed again and shook his head. "I thought it was safe. I really did. But . . ."

His voice trailed off. He closed his eyes again. "Someone . . ." he said finally. "Despite all my efforts . . . someone found its hiding place. Someone stole the book and ran into the forest with it."

I stared at Wendell. He was seriously upset. I could see this wasn't one of his wild stories. He was telling the truth.

"What's the book about?" I asked.

"Yes. Why is it so scary?" my sister demanded.

"I—I can't tell you," our uncle stammered. "It's so scary . . . I start to tremble just talking about it."

He wasn't lying. His hands were shaking. He tucked them into his pants pockets.

"If the book gets out . . ." he said, lowering his voice again to a whisper, ". . . if the book is opened . . . evil will be unleashed into the world. No one will be safe." He shivered. "No one's life will ever be the same."

Silence.

A long silence.

No one spoke. I kept hearing his whispered words. Hearing the fear in his voice.

"But . . . what can we do about it?" I asked finally.

"Find it," Wendell shot back. "Find it and lock it up again."

He took a deep, shuddering breath. "We must go into the forest—tomorrow morning. And we must get that book back—even if it *kills* us!"

A WARNING

My head was spinning as Betty and I made our way up the steep staircase to my room.

Betty followed me and closed the door behind her. She dropped down on the edge of the bed and raised her eyes to me. "So? What do you think?"

I shrugged. "Think? I don't know what to think."

"Is he for real?" Betty said. "Mom said he was a storyteller."

"He sure seemed serious," I said. "I don't think he was kidding around."

She thought about it for a moment. "Come on, Billy," she said finally. "How scary can a book be? Scary enough to send evil into the world? He makes it sound like everyone on earth will be destroyed if we don't get that book back."

"I've read a lot of scary books," I said. "But mostly they were fun. I mean, you get creeped out for a little while. Then you get over it. And there's usually a happy ending."

"So maybe he's making it up?" she said. "I mean, he didn't tell us what the book is about."

"Maybe it's too scary," I replied. "Maybe it's so scary, he can't even talk about it."

Betty shook her head. "It doesn't make sense."

I started to cross the room to my closet. "It doesn't matter. He's taking us into the forest tomorrow morning to find the book thief."

"That's another thing," Betty said, jumping to her feet. "Do you believe all that stuff about the forest being filled with dangerous prehistoric animals?"

I shrugged again. "I don't know what to think. I guess we'll find out."

She shivered. "What if we tell him we don't want to go?"

"You don't want to go?" I said. "Did you forget *you're* the brave one?"

She opened her mouth to answer. But we both turned as a huge shadow swept over our heads.

I ducked. A whoosh of air ruffled my hair.

Betty ducked, too, as the shadow shot over the room.

"It's a bat!" I cried. "It—it's so big! As big as a hawk!"

Flapping its wide wings, the creature dove at Betty. She dropped to her knees beside the bed, and it soared back up to the ceiling.

I shielded my head with both arms. The huge bat spread its wings and uttered an angry *screech*. It floated above us, bobbing in the air, wings flapping gently.

I stared up at it, my whole body shaking. "Oh no!" A cry escaped my mouth. "No. Oh no! Betty—look!"

She saw it, too—and let out a loud gasp.

The bat—*it had a tiny HUMAN head!*

"Are you KIDDING me?!" Betty shouted.

I blinked several times. I knew I had to be imagining it.

But no. The eyes . . . the mouth . . . the face . . .

A bat with a human head!

It stared down at us and let out another screech.

Then it lowered its head, flapped its wings hard—and came swooping down at me.

I raised my arms to cover my hair. I felt the flutter of wings close to my face.

I opened my eyes and saw the creature's lips moving. Its *human* lips.

"Get out!" the bat whispered. *"Get out!"*

"It talks! Noooooo!" A scream escaped my throat.

Betty ducked as the bat swooped over her head.

And then I heard running footsteps.

I lowered my arms in time to see Jesse dart into the room. As she burst in, the bat flapped up to the ceiling.

Jesse stretched out one hand—and it swooped down and landed gently on her arm. *As if it was trained.*

She spun around and carried the giant bat to the open window. With a wave of her arm, she sent it flying out of the room. Then she turned back to us. "Are you okay?"

Betty and I were both shaking. I was breathing hard, and I could feel my heartbeat thudding in my chest. I took a deep breath and held it.

"That bat—" Betty started, pointing to the window. "Its head. It—"

"It's a manbat," Jesse said. "One of the creatures of the Wayward Forest."

"It—it attacked us!" I stammered.

"I'm sorry. I didn't mean to leave the window open," Jesse said. "The manbats . . . they don't usually come close to the house."

"But—but—" I sputtered. "It whispered words. It whispered for us to get out."

Jesse's eyes narrowed. Her voice lowered to a whisper. "Forget it," she said. "You're not going to listen to a bat—are you?"

MYSTERIOUS SOUNDS FROM THE SHED

Betty and I stared at her. "But—but—" I sputtered again.

Jesse opened her mouth to say something. But she stopped when Wendell stepped into the room.

"What is happening here?" he asked. He frowned at her. "Jesse, honey, I thought you were in the kitchen. What are you doing up here?"

"A manbat flew into Billy's room," she answered. "I—I chased it away."

Wendell snickered. "Those things are harmless," he said. "They are creepy, but they're harmless." He turned to Betty and me. "I hope that's the most dangerous creature you meet in Wayward Forest."

The next morning, Uncle Wendell led us out of the house. It was a gray morning with dark clouds hanging low over the trees. I zipped my jacket against the cool breeze.

A wide back lawn led to the thick line of trees in the near distance. The start of Wayward Forest. The tall grass bent one way, then the other in the shifting wind. Tiny white insects buzzed like clouds over the grass.

As we started to follow Wendell toward the trees, I saw three small wooden sheds in a line along one side of the lawn.

"Hey—!" I heard barking. Then Bellamy appeared at the shed in the middle, his long chain leash tied to a hook. He strained against the leash.

"Bellamy! There you are!" Betty cried. She went running to the dog, and I followed. He pulled at the chain leash, eager to get to us.

We both dropped to our knees in the grass to pet him.

"You have your own little doghouse," I said. I laughed as he licked my face. He was so glad to see us. His tail whipped back and forth, and he made excited *yip* sounds as he jumped on us.

Uncle Wendell stayed in the middle of the yard. "You'll have plenty of time to spend with your dog," he said. "Let's get moving. The book thief has a big lead on us."

I wanted to stay and play with Bellamy. "Can we bring him along?" I asked. Of course, I knew the answer.

"That dog won't last ten minutes in the Wayward Forest," Wendell said. "If an animal doesn't get him, a *plant* will eat him."

Excuse me? A dog-eating plant?

Why was Wendell really leading us into this kind of danger?

He shifted his large backpack on his shoulders. Then he waved for us to follow him.

Betty and I said good-bye to Bellamy and climbed to our feet. I glanced across the lawn at the other two sheds. Were they for garden equipment or something?

There was no time to check them out. We had to hurry to catch up to our uncle, who was taking long strides toward the forest.

The tall grass made a whooshing sound as it brushed against the legs of our jeans. The trees up ahead cast deep purple shadows over the ground.

"Stay close," Wendell said. His backpack bounced on his shoulders. He leaned forward as he walked, as if we were in a race. "Don't fall behind. You need to remember . . ."

I didn't hear the rest of what Wendell said because of the loud noise behind us. Banging sounds. And a shrill animal cry.

I spun around. The sounds seemed to be coming from the shed to the right of Bellamy. The dog stood stiff and alert. His eyes were on that shed.

Betty moved close to me. We heard another cry. More banging.

"Wendell, what is that?" I demanded. "Is someone in that shed?"

THE EGG IS HATCHING!

Wendell shook his head. "I trapped a bloodskeet a few days ago," he said. "I'm keeping it in there until I figure out how to get it back in the forest without it attacking me."

Bang bang bang.

The creature really wanted to get out.

"What's a bloodskeet?" Betty asked.

"It's a mosquito the size of a basketball," Wendell answered. "Try to picture it. It can suck all the blood from your body in less than two minutes."

I shivered. *Could that be true?* "I'm going to have nightmares about that," I said.

Betty laughed. "Billy always has nightmares about things that happen to him during the day. I never do. I never have bad dreams."

Betty loves telling people things like that about me. She thinks she's more mature because she's older.

"Sometimes he screams in his sleep," Betty told Wendell.

"That's a lie!" I cried. "That only happened once. When I got my foot caught in the bed."

Bang bang bang.

Wendell didn't smile. "I hope you won't have nightmares after our time in the forest," he said. "But I'm being honest with you. I'm telling you how scary it is because you might want to turn back. But you can't turn back. Just keep remembering we are saving the world from that book."

Whoa.

Wendell kept his gaze on the shed where the banging and cries continued.

"Stay out of those sheds," he said. "That's where I keep the dangerous creatures I catch."

He turned toward the trees. "Let's go. We're wasting time."

"Do you have a weapon?" I asked. "You know. To protect against these wild animals?"

He swung his long backpack around. "Here is my only weapon," he said. He dug his hand into the backpack and pulled out a long knife.

"It's a machete," he said, raising it in front of him so we could see it. "It's the only protection I need."

He slid it into his belt. "Okay. Let's move. We're ready for the forest now."

The high tree branches stretched over each other, so tangled and tight, they formed a roof over the forest. The branches blocked out the sunlight, making the forest nearly as dark as night.

Our shoes sank into the soft dirt path that twisted through the trees. I kept mopping sweat off my forehead, even though the air was cool.

I was surprised at how noisy the forest was. Shrill animal cries sounded all around us. And I could hear the brush and scrape of creatures darting through the thick shrubs on both sides of the path.

Wendell didn't have to warn me to keep close again. I *wanted* to stay as close to him as I could. All my senses were alert to danger. We couldn't see the creatures, but they were definitely all around us.

Were any of them friendly?

I didn't want to hang around to find out.

The path led us into a narrow clearing. I stared at a

pile of white round rocks at the edge of the open space. "Wendell, how did those big rocks get there?" I asked. "They're so shiny."

I ran over to the pile and rubbed my hand over one of the rocks. "It's really smooth," I said. "And it feels warm."

Wendell shook his head. "Those aren't rocks, Billy. They're eggs."

Craaaaack.

The sound from under my hand made me leap back.

Craaaack craaaack.

"What's happening?" I cried. "What's inside these eggs?"

Wendell's hand tightened on my shoulder. "We . . . we're about to find out," he said. He pointed. "Get back, Billy! That egg is hatching."

Another long *craaaack.* And the egg split open.

A large black head with glistening silver eyes poked out. And as the creature slowly appeared . . .

. . . our screams rang through the trees.

10

CANNIBALS

As I stared, the shell crumbled and fell apart. And a tall black bird staggered out onto the path, flapping wide wings.

It shook itself, sending wet slime splashing off it. Tested its legs. Turned its long, curled beak toward us.

Haw haw hawwww.

The bird made its first sounds. Harsh. Loud. Not friendly.

Larger than a turkey, it took awkward, thudding steps. Its head tilted to one side, the creature kept one silvery eye locked on us.

Craaaaack.

Another shell fell apart. Another huge black bird toppled out, flapping its wide wings.

Hawww hawww.

"Cannibal crows!" Wendell cried. "The eggs are all hatching now!"

"Sh-shouldn't we run?" I stammered.

Both birds lowered their heads and thudded toward us.

"Wendell—should we run?"

Betty and I started to back away. But Wendell held us in place. "Watch," he murmured.

The enormous crows raised their wings high, preparing to attack.

"Just watch," Wendell whispered.

The birds' cries turned to ferocious *squawwwwks.*

"No! Please!" I shouted.

I stared, trembling, as the birds turned on each other. Squawking, shrieking, beating their wings, they tore at each other with curled talons, and sank their open beaks again and again into one another.

"They're cannibals," Wendell said calmly. "They won't eat humans. They only eat each other."

The fierce fight was over in minutes. The two birds had torn each other apart and lay in pieces on the grass. Behind them, more eggs began to crack open.

"Let's go," Wendell said. "We've seen enough." He led us back on the path.

We trotted along the trail for a while. I kept glancing back to see if any of the giant crows were following us.

The path curved into a thick patch of trees. Wendell stopped. He stooped to the ground and examined the dirt near his feet. "Yes," he said, letting the dirt slip through his fingers. He slowly stood. "The book thief definitely came this way."

"Good," Betty said. "Do you think we're close? Will we be able to find him before dark? How do you plan to catch him? Will we be able to get back to the house tonight?"

The questions tumbled out. She didn't take a breath.

Wendell raised a finger to his lips. "Let's pick up the pace," he said. "Yes, I think we may be close."

"But if we catch up to him—?" I started. And then I sneezed. A thunderclap of a sneeze.

I opened my mouth to sneeze again. But the sneeze caught in my mouth as something heavy crashed onto my head.

"Unnnnh." A groan escaped my throat.

A big creature slammed down over my shoulders. And pain shot through my body as I crumpled facedown into the dirt.

11

DON'T SHOW ANY FEAR

"Unnnnh." I groaned again. I struggled to raise my head. I spit dirt from my mouth.

The heavy creature hunched on my back, holding me down.

"Unnnnh. Ohhhh." I couldn't breathe. I couldn't move.

Calling up all my strength, I heaved my body hard and rolled over. The creature toppled off with an angry roar.

Gasping for air, I leaped to my feet. "Why aren't you helping me?" I cried to Wendell and Betty.

They stood wide-eyed, arms outstretched. Were they preparing to help me? Or to run?

The big animal roared again and raised up on two feet. Was it a bear? A bear that had crashed down from a tree?

The creature stood taller than me, covered in black

fur, a long snout, jaws opening and closing. Its furry chest heaved in and out.

"An arboreus-orso!" Wendell exclaimed. "A flying tree bear. They live in the high branches. They walk on two legs, but we call them flying bears because they swing from tree to tree. They grab their prey and carry it to the top branches to devour it."

"Huh?" I cried. A wave of panic shook my body. "Am I its prey?"

Wendell didn't answer.

The bear raised its claws and pawed the air with them. It pulled its lips back in an angry snarl.

"Your sneeze brought it down to the ground. He's just protecting his territory," Wendell explained.

"He . . . he can *have* his territory!" I cried. "I don't want it!"

"You startled it, and it wants to fight," Wendell said. Finally, he reached for his machete. But he made no effort to pull it out.

"Wh-what do I *do*?" I cried.

Wendell put a hand on my trembling shoulder. "Don't scream or shake, Billy. And don't sneeze again. Don't show him any fear. Or . . ."

"Or—?" I cried.

"Or he'll rip you in half and carry you up the tree."

The bear tilted its head back and let out a roar.

"He's definitely challenging you," Wendell said. "Stop shaking. Don't let him see your fear. Stop sweating!"

The bear stabbed a claw at me. Its body tensed. It was preparing to charge.

I grabbed the handle of Wendell's machete. "What about *this*?" I cried. "Why don't you take this out and—"

"It will only make him more angry," Wendell said. He slid the handle from my hand.

"Wh-what should I do?" I stammered in a high, shrill voice.

"Stare him down," Wendell answered.

"Huh?"

"Stare at him. Stare into his eyes. He'll retreat. He'll go back up in his tree."

"My legs . . . I can't stop shaking," I said. I wiped sweat from my forehead with the back of one hand.

"Stare at him," Wendell instructed. "Stare and keep staring." Wendell backed away.

I tried to stare into the bear's eyes. But my whole face was quivering and shaking. My teeth were chattering.

I saw the creature blink. It tensed its body and stretched to its full height. It opened its jaws in a low roar.

It saw. It saw my fear.

It didn't make another sound. Just arched its body. Raised both claws. And leaped at me.

12

A SNAKE BITE

I froze. No time to move or even scream.

Wendell sailed off his feet. He dove forward and tackled me to the ground.

The roaring tree bear hurtled toward us—and we rolled away. The bear crashed into a tree—so hard, the trunk shook. The creature landed on its belly in the dirt and didn't move.

Wendell scrambled to his feet. He pulled me up by one hand and pointed deeper into the forest. "Quick. Let's move!" he cried.

He led the way, running fast. Betty followed, her footsteps pounding the dirt. My legs felt shaky and weak, and my head was still spinning from fright. But I stumbled after them.

I kept looking back. Was the tree bear coming after us?

"Don't worry about it," Wendell called without turning around. "They seldom venture far from their tree."

As we followed the twisting path, the high tree branches continued to shut out almost all the light. Our shoes thudded and scraped over a thick carpet of dead leaves and weeds.

A throbbing pain in my side made me slow down. Wendell stopped and walked over to me, breathing hard. He wiped sweat from his beard. Then he put a hand on my shoulder.

"Billy, take a few deep breaths," he said. "We can't slow down. I don't think the thief has gone far. He may be just up ahead. We can catch him if we keep up the pace."

"Billy can never keep up with me," Betty said. "I can always outrun him."

"Betty—this is not the best time to be bragging," I said, still struggling to catch my breath.

She shrugged. "Just saying."

Wendell tugged me forward with both hands. "Let's go. We can decide who is the better runner later."

We began trotting over the path. Wendell led the way, with Betty close behind him. The wet leaves slid under my shoes. I stumbled a few times, but I caught my balance and kept up with them.

We followed a sharp turn in the path. Then it curved between a line of tall evergreens. Birds called to each other, trilling in deep tones, from the high branches of the trees. A long, furry animal darted across our path, running too quickly to see.

"The thief won't be in a hurry," Wendell said, without turning around. His shoes pounded the ground. "He won't know we're coming after him."

The narrow path curved sharply again. It was suddenly covered in flat, white pebbles.

"Whoooa!" I let out a cry as I stumbled over something. I saw it as I fell to the ground.

A tree root? A thick, white root poking up over the path.

I hit the pebbles hard on my elbows and knees.

And then I let out another startled cry.

The tree root—it moved!

Wendell and Betty spun around and stared down at me.

The root seemed to grow longer. It slid around my knees, holding me to the ground. It rose over me, and I saw its face.

"It's a snake!" I screamed. "Not a root! Not a root!"

It wrapped around me. Tighter. Tighter. I wasn't strong enough to pull free.

And then—to my horror—as its face inched closer to mine, its skin started to bulge and a second snake head appeared right next to the first. *The snake grew a second head!*

The second head snapped its jaws. Drool oozed from it curled fangs.

And then it happened again—and a *third* head poked out. It swung over me, dark eyes wide, hissing loudly.

All three mouths opened in a long *hisssss.* Then the middle head bolted forward—and stabbed its fangs into my chest.

13

"UNCLE WENDELL? WHERE ARE YOU?"

I toppled back—and the snake's fangs snagged my T-shirt and ripped a long tear in it.

Clicking their jaws, the other two heads arched over me, preparing to attack together.

I gasped in surprise as Betty darted forward in a blur. She shot out one hand and wrapped it around the snake behind the three heads.

"OFF!" she screamed. She yanked the snake off me—and heaved it into the trees.

We heard the clatter of leaves as it landed. We stared at each other, breathing noisily.

Betty leaned over me. "Are you okay?" Her voice came out in a hoarse whisper.

I shook my head. "Everything in this forest wants to kill us," I said.

Betty nodded. She fingered my ripped T-shirt. "Close one," she murmured. "You were outnumbered."

“I guess I should thank you,” I said.

“I guess you should,” she replied. Then she reached for my arm. “Get up. We can’t stay here. There might be more three-headed snakes.”

She helped me up. I squinted down the path, looking for more snakes pretending to be roots.

Then I turned to Wendell. “Hey—”

He wasn’t there.

“Hey—Wendell? Wendell?” I called.

Betty’s eyes went wide. “Where *is* he?”

We both took a few steps. I peered over a group of evergreen shrubs. “Wendell? Wendell—where’d you go?” Betty called.

I turned to her. My mouth suddenly felt dry. “He—he’s gone,” I stammered.

14

LIKE SOMETHING IN A HORROR MOVIE

"Did he go on without us?" I asked. "Didn't he see that snake attack me?"

Betty started to jog along the path. She waved for me to follow. "We have to catch up to him," she called to me.

"No. Wait—" I shouted. "He'll come back to get us. He has to."

"He's chasing the book thief," Betty said. "He won't come back. I'm sure he wants us to follow him."

"But he didn't tell us to follow him," I said. "He—he didn't say anything. He just took off without us."

I suddenly had a heavy feeling in the pit of my stomach. We'd been in the forest for a long time. The sun was already starting to lower behind the trees.

"Maybe he's waiting for us to run after him," Betty said.

"But . . . we don't know what's up ahead," I said, my voice shaking. "It's getting dark, Betty. We won't be able to see snakes or animals or—"

She narrowed her eyes at me. "So you just want to stand here and wait for Wendell to come back?"

I nodded. "Yes. I think we should. I think we should wait till—"

I stopped when I heard the scream. A shrill howl of pain—in the distance, up ahead of us. A long, high scream like something in a horror movie.

"Uncle Wendell?" Betty and I both cried at once.

STABBED

Silence.

I froze. Not moving, not breathing.

Listening.

Silence.

The birds had stopped trilling and chirping.

Betty and I stared at each other. I dug my hands deep into my jeans pockets. She crossed her arms in front of her.

More silence.

"Was that Wendell screaming like that?" Betty whispered.

I didn't answer. I started to run along the path. "We've got to find out," I said.

We ran side by side. In the dim light, we saw two more white root snakes across the path. We leaped over them and kept running.

The bird cries were back now, as if the danger had

passed. And I could hear the scrape and rustle of animals moving through the shrubs on both sides of the trail.

"Wendell? Can you hear us? Wendell?" I shouted.

No reply.

"That had to be him screaming," Betty said. "It wasn't an animal cry. It was human."

"If he's in trouble, we'll find him," I said.

Around another curve. "Oh!" I stopped so suddenly, I nearly toppled forward.

Betty saw it, too.

In the middle of the path. Was it an animal? Another snake?

I squinted into the gray light until it came into focus.

A machete. Wendell's machete. Standing straight up, the blade stabbed into the dirt.

"Wendell? Wendell?" My shouts came out high and shrill. I cupped my hands around my mouth and shouted some more.

No answer.

Betty and I stared at the machete. I wondered if she felt as afraid as I did.

Something had happened to Wendell. Something very bad.

Here was his only weapon. Left stabbed into the dirt.

I started to pull it from the ground. But it was buried deep. I stopped trying and backed away from it.

A bird cawed loudly in a tree limb above us. That set the other birds cawing all around us.

"Th-they're telling us to leave the forest," I stammered.

"I don't think so," Betty said. She put a hand on my shoulder. "Get a grip, Billy. Don't start thinking the birds are talking to us."

"Get a grip?" I cried. "How can I get a grip? Here we are all alone in the middle of this strange forest. Everything here is trying to kill us. And Uncle Wendell is gone. He might be in terrible trouble—or worse."

"We can't panic," she said.

"We *have* to panic!" I cried.

I knew I was being the baby. Betty was the grown-up and I was the baby. But I didn't care. The birds were warning us to get out of there. I knew they were.

Bats with human heads . . . Long roots turning into snakes and stretching across the path . . . Bears about to swing down from the trees . . .

And what else? What else was waiting to threaten us in this horrifying forest?

"I'm n-not staying here," I stammered. "We have to go back to Wendell's house."

Betty stared at me. She had her hands to her cheeks. I could see she was thinking. "But Wendell—" she said finally.

"We can't help him," I said. "Maybe he's okay. If he comes looking for us, he'll know we went back to his house."

"I guess we'll be safer there," Betty said.

"Of *course* we'll be safer there," I replied. I tugged her arm. "Let's go. Before it's pitch-black out here."

We turned and started to walk back along the path. We took careful steps, keeping our heads down, watching for snakes.

The harsh calls of birds seemed to follow us. Leaves crackled and crunched as animals darted beside the path.

We stopped in a patch of thick grass.

"I—I don't see the path," I said. "Why didn't we bring a flashlight?"

"The path is all covered up," Betty said. "Or . . . did we somehow wander off it?"

I squatted down and rubbed both hands through the thick grass. "This . . . this isn't the path," I said. "We're not on the path."

"Then where *is* it?" Betty cried. Her turn to panic. She spun in a circle. "How did we lose it? Where is it?"

I couldn't answer. We stared at each other.

An animal uttered a low growl. Nearby.

"We—we're lost," I whispered. "Totally lost. How will we ever find our way?" I whispered.

Then I had an idea.

16

IS THERE SUCH A THING AS QUICKSAND?

"Maybe we could find shelter," Betty said. "It will be much easier to find the path in the morning."

"No. Wait," I said. I reached into my jeans pocket. "My phone. I have my phone. Why didn't I think of it?"

I gripped the phone tightly and held it up to show my sister.

"But . . . we don't have Wendell's number," she said.

"We don't need that," I replied. "I'll call 911. They can send someone to find us and—"

"What if there is no 911 out here?" Betty said. "What if—"

"I can call Mom and Dad," I said. "They will know how to get someone to find us."

"Well, go ahead," Betty said. She shivered. From the cold? Or from fear? She pushed my arm. "Hurry. Try it."

I raised the phone in front of me and stared into the glare of the screen. I started to press 911—then stopped.

I let out a groan. "Oh noooo."

Betty bumped up against my side. "What is it? What's wrong?"

"No bars," I said. "No anything. Look. It says *No Service*."

Betty sighed. "We should have known. The phone is useless."

"Well . . . at least we have a flashlight now," I said. I pressed the phone's light on.

In time to see a large creature swoop down from the trees.

Wings flapped loudly. It sounded like clapping hands.

I tilted the light to it. I saw its wide wings. And then the light fell on its head. On its face. Its *human* face.

Of course, I recognized it. A manbat.

It opened its mouth in a long shrill shriek. Then it dove at Betty, flapping hard.

Betty screamed and tossed her hands up, trying to swat the shrieking creature away.

But the manbat sank its claws into Betty's hair.

"Don't panic," I said. "Uncle Wendell said the manbats are harmless—remember?"

"Well . . . *no one told this manbat*!" she screamed.

The creature tugged her hair straight up. Betty swung both arms, trying to shove it away.

"Don't just stand there, Billy! *Help me!*"

"Wh-what can I do?" I stammered.

What can I do? What can I do?

I had the phone gripped tightly in my hand. An idea flashed into my mind. I raised the beam of light and aimed it at the manbat.

The light bounced off its wings and down its fat body. I moved the phone till I caught the creature's face in the beam. I saw its eyes go wide. The mouth opened in surprise.

The manbat blinked several times. Turned its head away. Its wings fluttered wildly.

I kept the light beam locked on it. The manbat shut its eyes and uttered a shrill shriek.

"Yes!" I cried. "It hates the light. Bats hate the light."

I kept the beam of light on its face. The creature flapped its wings hard and tried to lift off, tried to fly away.

But its talons were caught in the tangles of Betty's hair.

"Owww!" Betty screamed. She tugged frantically at her hair. "What are you doing? You made it WORSE!"

The bat shrieked, flapped its wings, and yanked my sister's hair. She slapped at it harder, trying to fling it away.

"Stop struggling!" I cried. I lowered the light and burst forward. I grabbed Betty's arms and held them down at her sides.

The bat gave one last screech and jerked free. We watched it soar into the trees.

Betty smoothed down her hair with both hands. Her whole body shuddered. She grabbed a tree trunk to hold herself up. "That . . . that was *horrible*," she choked out.

"I saved you," I said. "Score one for me."

"You didn't do anything," Betty snapped. "The bat wanted to get away and—"

"Not true!" I cried. "My light—"

I stopped when I felt something brush against my face. I swatted at it with one hand. Something bumped the back of my neck.

Betty brushed something off her shoulder. I swung the light on it and squinted to focus. Then they came clearly into view.

Moths!

Pale moths as big as robins!

Moths swarmed around us, poking us, bumping us, trying to land on us.

"See what you did, genius?" Betty cried. "Your light brought out all these moths! They are drawn to light—remember?"

I swatted at a swarm of the big insects.

"Turn off the light!" Betty cried. "Turn it *off*!"

I clicked the phone and the light went out. But the moths continued attacking us in the dark.

I dodged and ducked and swung my arms. But they swarmed over me, their thick wings scraping my face, my hair, the back of my neck.

"Owwww!" My sister's scream made me jump.

"They bite!" she cried. "Owwww. They're *biting* me! This is your fault, Billy!"

I tried to bat them off me with both hands. "Run!" I cried. "Maybe we can outrun them."

My shoes slid in the grass as I took off. Moths clung to my hair, my back, my shoulders as I tried to escape.

I could hear Betty's pounding footsteps as she followed. Heard her cries of pain as the big moths bumped and bit her and scraped her skin.

"They're going to eat us alive!" she cried.

"Keep running!" I shouted—and a big moth flew into my mouth. I started to choke on it.

I heard a splashing sound. My jeans legs suddenly felt wet against my skin. I glanced down. I was kicking up water and mud.

Water? Mud?

"Oh no," I murmured. I began to sink. Moths darted against my face. The mud—it was nearly up to my knees.

I tried to move, but I was stuck. And sinking fast.

I turned and saw Betty struggling, batting at the attacking moths as she twisted her body. Trying to pull herself forward in the muck.

"Billy, what's happening?" she cried. "We—we're sinking fast!"

The thick mud bubbled up around my waist. I felt as if I was being pulled down fast.

"Is there such a thing as quicksand?" I shouted. "If there is, we found it!"

A wide bubble popped up around me. Mud splashed over my head. And I sank under the warm, wet goo.

17

DON'T OPEN THE SHED DOOR!

I shut my eyes and held my breath. But mud oozed into my nose. I started to choke.

I felt myself sliding down, deeper into the muck.

Deeper.

Then, to my surprise, my shoes landed on something. Something hard.

Was it the bottom?

I forced my legs to move forward. Yes. I'd hit the bottom. The quicksand wasn't deep! We weren't going to drown.

My chest was already aching from lack of oxygen. But I pushed both arms above my head. Kicked hard against the bottom. And forced myself up.

I scissored my legs and swung my arms.

Yes. Yes.

My head bobbed over the surface. Eyes still shut, I

sucked in breath after breath. Then I wiped the mud off my face and eyes.

"Billy—there you are!" I heard my sister's cry.

I turned, sending up a wave of mud. Betty stood on the edge of the quicksand. She held a tree branch in her hands and shoved it across the mud at me.

"Grab onto it, Billy. I'll pull you out."

I grabbed the branch with both hands. "How—how did you get out so fast?" I stammered.

She pulled and pulled and tugged me out. "I'm a great swimmer, Billy. Do you think I got all those trophies for losing?" She shook her head.

"Okay. Two rescues for you," I said. "You're ahead."

We stood there covered in wet mud. "At least the moths are gone," I said.

She rolled her eyes. "That's you, Billy. Always looking on the bright side."

We found the path and followed it through the trees to Wendell's house. I crossed my fingers and hoped he'd be there when we got back.

But were we headed the right way? Or were we walking deeper into Wayward Forest?

The mud had dried and caked to my clothing. I hoped Wendell had a big bathtub. I was going to need at least *five* baths when I got to the house!

Betty and I both stopped when we heard noises above us in the trees. A low growl. Then another.

"Tree bears!" I exclaimed.

We heard the creak of the shifting branches and the low, muttered growls of the bears up above us.

"This is good news," Betty said, breathing hard. "It means this is the way we came. We're heading in the right direction."

"I—I hope so," I stammered. "Keep going. I don't want another wrestling match with one of them!"

It was night when we finally stepped out of the forest.

I wanted to cheer and jump for joy. But I barely had the strength to move another inch. I bent over, grabbed my muddy knees, and forced myself to take breath after breath.

"We . . . we made it," Betty said. She slapped me on the back and nearly knocked me over. "Look." She pointed.

Under the pale light of a full moon, Wendell's back lawn stretched in front of us. In the distance, I could see the house rising into the purple sky. And I could see the three sheds forming a shadowy line across the side of the lawn.

"Bellamy!" I said. "The poor guy must be lonely."

"I hope Jesse remembered to feed him," Betty said.

We both trotted through the tall grass, wet from the dew, toward Bellamy's shed. I stopped when I heard a cry. Betty stopped beside me and uttered a gasp.

We heard another shrill cry. And then banging sounds. From the shed on the right.

"The same as this afternoon," I said.

"Wendell said that he had caught something called a bloodskeet," Betty whispered. "But—"

"But the shouts are so human!" I said.

"Hellllp!"

"That's definitely a person," Betty said. "That's not an animal cry."

We stayed together and crept closer to the shed.

Bannng bannnnng.

I stopped.

Someone was in that shed. Pounding hard on the metal wall.

I pulled Betty back.

"We can't go near that shed," I whispered.

She swung free of my grasp. "Why not?"

"Wendell said not to, remember? He said to stay away."

"Well, Wendell isn't here," Betty replied. "And it sounds like someone is in trouble in there."

Bellamy started to bark.

"Let's go see Bellamy instead," I said. "Let's listen to what Wendell said and—"

Bannng bannnnng.

The beating on the shed wall drowned out Bellamy's barking.

"We're coming, Bellamy! Don't worry!" Betty shouted. But she trotted up to the shed at the end of the row.

I hung back. I knew this could be trouble. Wendell had warned us about the shed. And he seemed very serious.

Betty reached out and wrapped her hand around the padlock on the shed door.

"No—don't!" I cried, stepping up beside her. "Don't touch the lock. Please. We *can't* open the door. We can't!"

Betty ignored me. She gave the lock a hard tug—and it popped open.

“No!” I screamed. “Betty—don’t open the door. Let’s wait for Wendell. Don’t open it.”

She refused to listen. She grabbed the metal door handle—and yanked it open.

Then we both screamed in horror as a wild-eyed man roared out at us.

18

MISTAKEN IDENTITY?

I flung myself back, trying to get away. And I crashed into Betty. We both struggled to stay on our feet.

The man's chest heaved up and down as he sucked in breath after breath. His face was red and spotted with dirt. He swept back his long tangles of blond hair and mopped the sweat that ran off his forehead and the blond stubble on his cheeks.

He wore a loose-fitting white sweatshirt over baggy khaki pants. They were wrinkled and stained. Breathing hard, he stretched his arms above his head, a long stretch after being squeezed in the low shed.

Betty and I were frozen in surprise. I jumped as a burst of wind blew the shed door shut behind him.

"I . . . I . . . I . . ." His voice was hoarse from screaming. He raised his eyes to us and squinted, as if confused. He studied Betty for a long moment, then me.

"Billy?" he said finally. "Betty?" His voice was a harsh growl.

"You—you're here?"

I opened my mouth to answer. But no sound came out. My heart was still pounding in my chest.

"How do you know our names?" Betty demanded. "Who are you?"

The man swallowed. He made a sour face. His throat must have been sore.

"Of course I know your names," he said finally. "I'm your uncle Wendell."

PART TWO

19

MEET THE BOOKWORM

My head spun. I struggled to make sense of this.

Two Uncle Wendells?

No. One of them was a liar.

But how could Betty and I know which one was our real uncle? We were just babies the last time we saw him.

If only Mom and Dad had hung around. They would have known the real Wendell instantly.

If this man was lying, it meant we were both in real danger.

Betty and I stared at each other.

This "Wendell" motioned toward the house.

Did we have a choice? No. We had to follow him. We had to figure out what was going on here.

In the house, he went right to the kitchen and emptied the refrigerator. He pulled out half a turkey, a bowl of mashed potatoes, salad, a melon, and several bottles of iced tea. He found a loaf of bread in a drawer and carried it to the table with everything else.

Betty and I sat across from him and watched him gobble down everything. He just shoved it all into his open mouth and didn't even stop to chew.

I sat tensely across from him at the table. I stayed alert in case we had to jump up and run.

"Three days," he muttered, juice running down his chin. He swallowed a chunk of turkey. "I've been locked in that shed for three days." He raised a bottle of iced tea to his mouth and chugged it down.

"But—why?" I said. "Who—?"

"The thief," he answered. He wiped his mouth with the back of his hand. "The thief who is after the scariest book ever."

"He locked you in the shed?"

"He—he surprised me," Wendell said. "I thought I was safe living here at the edge of the forest, safe from intruders."

He sliced the melon in half and buried his face in it. "So hungry," he murmured. "Pardon my manners."

We waited until he slurped up the melon. He wiped the juice off his face with the sleeve of his sweatshirt.

"He knew I had the book well hidden," Wendell continued. "So he locked me away in the shed. That way, he could take all the time he needed to search for the book."

"Did he find it? Who is he? Is Jesse *your* daughter?" The questions spilled from Betty's mouth.

Wendell squinted at her. "Jesse? Who is Jesse? I don't have a daughter."

"She was here with him," I said. "She helped us chase away a manbat."

"She was helping *him*, not you," Wendell said. "Maybe Jesse is his daughter. Or maybe she only works for him."

"Who is he?" I repeated Betty's question.

Wendell shrugged. "I don't know his real name. He's known as 'the Bookworm.' Except he doesn't read books—he steals them."

My mind spun. This was almost too much to think about. The man who told us he was Uncle Wendell wasn't Uncle Wendell. He was the thief.

That is, if *this* man was telling the truth. *Should we believe him?*

"What did the Bookworm tell you?" Wendell asked. "Did he tell you he found the scary book?"

I shook my head. "No. He said the thief took the book and escaped into the forest."

"That's why we had to follow him there," Betty said. "He said we had to go into the forest to help him catch the thief."

Wendell sighed. "All a lie," he said. "He probably took you into the forest because he wanted to *lose* you there."

"Huh?" Betty and I both gasped.

"He figured you would never survive the Wayward Forest," Wendell said. "And he and that woman Jesse would be left alone in my house to search for the book."

Betty and I stared at him from across the table. I didn't know what to say. It was all too much to take in. I felt as if my head was about to explode.

Betty finally spoke. "But in the forest . . ." she started. "We heard him scream. Like he was in terrible trouble."

"And we found his machete on the path," I added.

"All a trick," Wendell said. "A trick to keep you searching for him while he came back to the house. He wanted you out of the way so he could steal the book."

I gasped again. "You mean—?"

"You mean he's here. He came back to the house?" Betty asked.

Before Wendell could answer, a loud *crash* from the front room made the three of us jump.

Wendell's eyes went wide. "Yes, he's here. The Bookworm is *back*!"

MORE LIES

Wendell leaped to his feet. He picked up a broom from the corner of the kitchen. He waved it as he raced for the front room.

Betty and I held back. A cold shiver shook my body. I forced myself to stand up. "Come on," I said. "We have to follow him. If he needs help . . ."

I stood in the kitchen doorway with Betty right behind me.

We listened, but we didn't hear any voices.

We tiptoed to the front room and found Wendell standing by an open window. He held the broomstick in one hand and gazed down at the floor.

"A lamp," he said. "It must have crashed to the floor. The wind probably knocked it over."

I realized I was holding my breath. I let it out in a long whoosh.

"So . . . we don't know if the thief is back in the house or not?" I said.

Wendell bent to pick up the lamp. Part of it had shattered into several jagged pieces. "I think we can expect him," he said. Wendell left the lamp pieces on the floor and went to close the window.

Then he dropped down on the long leather couch and set the broomstick at his feet. Betty and I slid into armchairs across from the couch.

"He'll be back," Wendell said. "I know he hasn't found the book."

"How do you know?" I asked. "Maybe he had it with him and ran off with it in the forest."

Wendell shook his head. "No way. I hid it too well."

"Well . . ." I started. "Is anything he told us true? Is it really the scariest book on earth? Is it really dangerous?"

Wendell swept a hand back through his blond hair. He glanced out the window, as if he was afraid someone might be listening. "That part is true," he said finally.

I swallowed. "Seriously?"

"I need to protect that book with my life," Wendell said in a low whisper. "I can't let it get out into the world. It would ruin many lives."

"What is it about?" Betty asked.

Wendell raised a finger to his lips. "Don't ask that question, Betty," he said. "I will not answer it."

He climbed to his feet. "Come with me," he said. "I'll show you where I hid the book. But don't ever go near it. And don't ever dare open it."

Betty and I stood up and followed him. To my surprise, he didn't lead us down to the basement or to some hidden room at the end of a long hall. He led us back to the kitchen.

He stopped at the bookshelf against one wall. The shelves went up to the ceiling. He turned and smiled at us. "I knew the Bookworm would never find the book if I hid it in plain sight," he said.

I gazed at the books on the shelves. They seemed to all be cookbooks.

"I slipped the book between my dessert cookbooks," he said. "I knew he would *never* think of looking here."

"Let me show you," Wendell said.

He reached up to a shelf just above his head.

"Hey—it's GONE!"

21

I'LL GIVE YOU TO THE COUNT OF THREE!

Betty and I uttered startled cries.

"You mean—?" I started.

Wendell's eyes were wide with fright. "Oh, wait." He slapped his forehead. "I forgot," he said. "I moved it to the appetizers books."

He wrapped his hand around a very thick black book. "Yes. Yes. Here it is." He pulled it out a few inches so we could see it clearly. Then he carefully pushed it back into place with the cookbooks.

He turned to us. "People have been trying to steal the book for many years," he said. "These are evil people who would like to see fear unleashed on the world."

"Why don't you just burn it?" Betty demanded. She always asks the questions I wouldn't dare ask.

"Burning it would unleash its evil," Wendell answered. "Destroying it would let its evil escape. The book cannot be destroyed. It must be kept closed and hidden away—forever."

Betty and I both nodded. We stared at the book a little longer.

"My family has lived here at the edge of the Wayward Forest for centuries," Wendell said. "We chose this home because we thought it was safe. It's our mission in life to protect the book. I will not let anyone take it—especially the Bookworm."

"Sorry to disagree," boomed a voice from the doorway.

With a cry, I spun around—and saw the Bookworm stride into the kitchen.

A wide smile stretched across his face under his black beard. "Thank you," he said, "for leading me right to the book, Wendell. I saw you had escaped the shed. I was hoping you would be foolish enough to help me like this."

"Now, wait—!" Wendell cried.

Jesse appeared behind the Bookworm. She raised a long metal object in front of her. "This is a flame-thrower," she said. "Don't move."

The Bookworm crossed the room to us. "If you give us any trouble," he said, "Jesse will flame your entire book collection." He narrowed his eyes at Wendell. "Do you understand?"

"I—I understand," Wendell stammered. "But, please—"

The thief stuck out a hand. "Just give me the book, Wendell, and there will be no trouble. You don't want your entire collection in ashes, do you?"

Betty and I exchanged glances. We both wanted to act, to do something to help Wendell. But we watched Jesse raise the flamethrower. We knew we were helpless.

The Bookworm's face was red, and his forehead was dripping with sweat. He stuck his hand out closer. "Give it to me," he growled. "Hurry."

Wendell had his hand on the book. "Listen to me," he said. "If you take this book, you will ruin the lives of millions of people. You will spread fear everywhere and—"

"No talking!" the thief boomed.

Jesse stepped forward with the flamethrower aimed at the bookshelf.

The Bookworm stuck his hand out again. "Wendell, I'll give you to the count of three to put the book in my hand." His dark eyes flashed. "One . . . two . . . three."

THE BOOKWORM WINS

I held my breath as Wendell wrapped his hand around the spine of the black book. He started to pull it out. Then he lowered his hand.

His fingers were shaking. His eyes were blinking rapidly. He was breathing through his open mouth.

He grabbed the book again. But then let go of it. "I—I just can't do it," he stammered.

Jesse stepped closer with the flamethrower. Her eyes narrowed. She had her jaw clenched tightly, as if ready for battle.

The Bookworm shook his head. "Wendell," he said softly, "think of your niece and nephew. They'd hate to be caught in a burning inferno."

Wendell uttered a gasp.

"Think of them," the thief said. "Think of their young lives."

Jesse tilted the flamethrower up, aimed at the cookbook shelves.

"Okay, okay!" Wendell cried. He tugged the black book from the shelf and held it out for the Bookworm to take. "Here. It's yours. But I'm warning you—"

The thief snatched it from Wendell's hand. "No more warnings," he growled. He pressed the book close to his chest.

"You've lost, Wendell," he said. "You're a loser. The two kids see what a loser you are." A smile crossed his face. "And now you have a fire to put out."

He nodded to Jesse.

She sent a fiery blast to the bookshelf. And the cookbooks burst into crackling orange and yellow flames.

RETURN OF THE BOOKWORM

"Nooooo!" Wendell screamed. He put his hands on our backs and shoved Betty and me away from the fire.

Flames crackled and sizzled as the books caught fire. Black smoke rose to the ceiling.

Jesse was already out the kitchen door. The Bookworm gave one last look at the burning shelves. Then he spun away and ran after her.

"Get down!" Wendell shouted to us. "You're still too close!"

My sister and I ducked our heads and stumbled forward. Black smoke billowed around us. I tried to hold my breath. But my eyes burned and I started to choke.

Wendell dove to the cabinets under the kitchen sink. He pulled open door after door. "Where is it? Where is it?" he cried. Finally, he pulled out a small red fire extinguisher.

He raised it to the darting flames and sent a long

stream of foam over the shelves. The flames sputtered loudly, struggling to stay alive. But the fire was out in a few seconds. Clouds of black smoke filled the kitchen.

Wendell kept his eyes on the blackened shelves, making sure the fire was out. Then he dropped the fire extinguisher to the floor and waved for us to follow him.

"Are you okay?" he asked as we made our way along the front hall. He handed me a handkerchief to wipe the burning tears from my eyes. I took a breath and tried to stop choking on the smoke.

"I'm okay. But my heart is still beating like crazy," Betty said.

Wendell led us to the front room and dropped back onto the couch where we had been a short while earlier. He let out a long sigh. "Well . . . that went well," he said sarcastically.

Betty and I sat across from him.

He shut his eyes and rubbed them. Then he rested his head on the back of the couch.

I stared hard at him. Why was he so calm? Why wasn't he more upset?

"Are you going to chase after him?" I asked.

"Aren't you going to try to get the book back?" my sister demanded.

A strange smile spread over Wendell's mouth. "I don't think so," he said softly.

"But—but—" I sputtered. "He's running away with the book!"

"It's a fake," Wendell said.

"Huh? It's *what*?" I cried.

"It's a fake," he repeated. "It's not the real book." He leaned forward. "You don't think I'd be dumb enough to leave the real book on a cookbook shelf—do you?"

Betty and I stared at him. We were both trying to deal with what he was telling us.

"I knew the Bookworm was listening," Wendell said. "I saw his footprints here in the front room. The wind didn't knock that lamp over. *He* did."

"You knew the Bookworm was here the whole time?" I said.

He nodded. "So I led him into the kitchen. I always have that black book ready. Just in case somebody tries to steal the real one."

"Wow. That's amazing!" I shook my head.

"Billy and I were really scared—" Betty started.

"I didn't have a chance to tell you the truth," Wendell said. "I'm really sorry. But I was eager to fool the Bookworm."

"Well, where *is* the real scary book?" Betty asked.

Wendell climbed up from the couch. "I'll show you," he said.

He led us down a back hall, around a corner, and down another long hall. At the basement stairs, he clicked on a ceiling light, and we followed him down, our shoes clanging on the metal steps.

"Betty and I have been down here," I said.

Wendell didn't reply. He opened a narrow door. I could see another steep stairway going down.

"There is a second basement," he said. "A basement under the basement."

Again, our shoes clanged on the metal steps. I gripped the slender banister tightly. The steps were really steep and narrow, and I didn't want to fall.

We followed Wendell deeper underground. The air was cool down here, much cooler than the first basement, and dry. Wendell clicked on a ceiling light. It threw pale light over a large room where bookshelves were lined up in rows, just like in our school library.

"I have to keep a cool temperature here," Wendell said. "I keep my most valuable books in this basement."

He walked to the wall and pressed a round black button cut into the stone. "Here's another secret," he said.

I heard a rumbling sound. The stones in the wall slid apart, and a tall, gray metal box rolled into view. "My hidden safe," Wendell said.

The safe was wider and taller than a refrigerator. It was at least eight feet tall.

Wendell tapped the side with his fist. "Solid steel," he said.

I ran my hand over the side of the safe. The metal felt smooth and cool.

"The book is hidden in this safe," Wendell said. He spun the dial on the front. "I'm the only one who knows how to open the wall to bring out the safe. And I'm the only one who knows the combination."

"And now you're going to share it with *me*!" called a voice from the stairwell.

I heard the clatter of footsteps. Turned. And saw the Bookworm taking the stairs two at a time.

Striding quickly toward us, he scowled at Wendell. "You didn't think you could fool me with that phony book in the kitchen—*did* you?"

24

ANOTHER BIG SURPRISE

"I—I—" Wendell started to choke, his eyes wide in surprise.

Another clatter of footsteps brought Jesse down to the basement. She hoisted the flamethrower and pointed it at Wendell.

Betty and I backed away to the far wall. Wendell stood open-mouthed, his hand still on the safe.

"Listen to reason," Wendell pleaded.

Jesse waved the flamethrower. "Shall we have a barbecue?" she asked the Bookworm. "Wendell, medium-rare."

"No, please—!" Wendell cried.

She tilted the flamethrower up and sent a burst of flames into the air. The roar echoed off the basement walls.

"I should have known. A hidden safe!" the Bookworm

said. “Hand us the book. The real book this time. And we won’t harm you.”

“But—but—” Wendell sputtered.

Betty and I huddled against the wall. My legs felt as wobbly as rubber bands. I had to force myself to breathe.

Jesse kept waving the flamethrower up and down, ready to fire it again.

“I’m not a bad person,” the Bookworm said. “I just love to collect books. Book collectors can’t be bad people, can they?”

“You know what you’re doing is wrong,” Wendell said. “You know the evil power of this book. You know—”

“ENOUGH TALK!” the Bookworm screamed. “Open the safe—now. Or you’ll be Smoked Wendell. I’m not playing games!”

A sigh escaped Wendell’s lips. “Okay, okay,” he murmured.

He glanced at Betty and me. I could see the sadness in his eyes. His chin twitched with fear.

His hand shook as he reached for the dial on the front of the safe. He started to turn the dial. “I—I can’t do it,” he stammered. “My hand is trembling too hard.”

“Try harder,” the thief growled. “Jesse is getting impatient. She loves a good fire.”

Wendell gritted his teeth and turned the dial. It made soft clicks as he spun it to the combination.

He sighed again and stopped. He reached for the door handle. He wrapped his fingers around the handle and slowly tugged the door open.

"Whoooaaa!"

We all screamed as we stared into the safe—*and saw that it was completely empty.*

LAUGHTER

The Bookworm stared into the empty safe. "What kind of trick is this?" he cried.

He grabbed the flamethrower from Jesse's hands. With a growl, he raised it—and jabbed it into Wendell's belly.

Wendell groaned, grabbed his stomach, and started to collapse to the floor.

"Stop it!" I cried. "Leave him alone!"

"I can't take any more tricks," the Bookworm shouted, threatening to jab Wendell again. "I want that book—now!"

Wendell raised both hands in surrender. "Enough," he whispered. "Enough."

He backed up against the wall beside Betty and me. "Enough," he said again. "I have to tell you the truth."

The Bookworm kept the flamethrower raised. "Yes, you have to. And quickly."

"No more lies about the book," Wendell said. "Listen to me carefully, Bookworm. It doesn't exist."

"What?" Jesse cried.

The Bookworm narrowed his eyes at Wendell and took a step closer to him. "Say that again?"

"It doesn't exist," Wendell repeated. "There's no such thing as the scariest book ever. I made it up."

The Bookworm rolled his eyes. "Can't you stop lying?"

"I—I'm not lying," Wendell stammered. "I made the whole thing up."

"Why?" the thief demanded.

"I made it up because I wanted to be famous," Wendell answered. "I wanted my book collection to be famous. I wanted people to know me."

The Bookworm rubbed his black beard. His eyes locked on Wendell. "You made up the book to be famous?"

Wendell nodded. "I wanted to be known around the world as the owner of the scariest book ever. But—but—" His voice broke. "It's all a lie. There is no scariest book ever—except in my imagination."

Wendell lowered his eyes and stared at the floor.

The Bookworm gazed at him for a long while. And then to my shock, he tossed back his head and burst out laughing.

LOCKED IN

The Bookworm's laughter rang off the stone basement walls. Jesse stood behind him, her face serious, her eyes on the empty safe.

When he finally stopped laughing, the thief wiped tears from his beard. He grinned at Wendell. "You're such a terrible liar, Wendell," he said. "If the book doesn't exist, why did you tell the kids about it?"

"And why did you bring them to this basement?" Jesse chimed in. "Why do you have this safe in the wall if there is no scary book?"

The Bookworm laughed again. "Should we give you time to come up with a better lie?"

Wendell shook his head. "Don't believe me? You can search forever. But you'll never find the book."

"I *am* going to search for it," the Bookworm replied. "Every corner of your house from top to bottom. And I'm going to find it."

He turned to Jesse. "Do *you* believe Wendell's story?"

"Of course not," she answered. "The book is somewhere in this house. It *has* to be."

Betty and I exchanged glances. *Is Wendell telling the truth? Did he really make up the whole idea of the scariest book ever? Or is he just trying to get the two thieves to leave?*

I couldn't decide.

And it didn't really matter what Betty and I thought. The Bookworm and Jesse were not going away.

But what were they going to do with us?

I quickly found out.

The Bookworm raised the flamethrower. "Get into the safe," he said. "All three of you."

"Huh?" Betty gasped. "What do you mean?"

"I mean get into the safe," the thief growled, waving the flamethrower. "Jesse and I don't want to be disturbed while we search for the book."

"But—but—" I stammered.

"We won't be able to breathe in there," Betty said.

He scowled at her. "Is that *my* problem?"

"Let the kids go," Wendell said. "I'll go into the safe. Leave them out. They won't bother you."

"They're *already* bothering me," the Bookworm

said. He laughed at his own joke. "Get in. Now. I'm not kidding around."

"But—are you going to come back and let us out?" I stammered.

He shrugged. "Maybe. Depends on what kind of mood I'm in."

I stared into the safe. This was going to be a very tight squeeze.

"There *is* no book," Wendell repeated. "You've got to believe me."

"Sure. Just like I believe pigs can fly," the thief said.

He jabbed the flamethrower into Wendell's chest. "MOVE!" he screamed.

Jesse grabbed his shoulder. "Don't hurt them," she said. "Let's just find the book and get out of here. This house gives me the creeps."

Wendell sighed and stepped into the open safe. "You're making a terrible mistake," he said. "If anything happens to these kids . . ."

"I won't be around to know about it," the Bookworm said. "I'll be far away from here with a new book to add to my collection."

He pointed the flamethrower at Betty and me.

We had no choice. I stepped into the safe and she followed me.

The three of us stared out at the Bookworm and Jesse. The safe was so narrow, our shoulders touched. With a sigh, Wendell pushed in between us.

“Please—” Wendell started.

But the heavy door slammed shut. We were locked in darkness.

DON'T PANIC

After the slam of the safe door, nothing but a ringing silence. All I could hear was my breathing, loud and rapid, as if I'd just run a mile. The darkness felt thick, heavy as a blanket.

"Billy," Wendell whispered, so close to my ear, I could feel his hot breath on my face. "Billy, don't panic. Try to breathe normally. Slow . . . slow breaths."

"You're using up all the air!" Betty said.

"Don't panic?" I cried. "Did you really say don't panic? It's already hot in here. I'm drenched in sweat. And how much air do we have? What if he doesn't come back to let us out?"

"Don't panic," Wendell whispered. I felt his hand on my shoulder. "I have this under control."

That made me laugh. Despite my fear, I actually laughed.

"We're locked in this safe, maybe forever," I said. "And you have it under control?"

"Shhhhh," he hissed. "Quiet. Let's all be silent for a little while. Give them a chance to leave the basement. I know what I'm doing. Really."

I took a deep breath and tried to hold it. Drops of sweat ran down my forehead. My legs started to ache. But there was no room to sit down.

"Oh nooo," I moaned. "I'm going to sneeze." I pressed my fingers around my nose and tried to hold it in. But I couldn't.

The sneeze sounded like a fireworks explosion in the tiny safe.

"Billy—please!" Betty cried, shoving me. "You got it all over me!"

"S-sorry," I stammered.

How long would the three of us have to stand here, pressed together in this box? Would the Bookworm come back to rescue us?

And . . . why wasn't Wendell more upset?

A few silent minutes went by. They seemed like hours.

I tried to take slow breaths. But there was no way I could slow the *beat-beat-beat* of my heart.

"Okay. I think they're gone," Wendell whispered. "Let's get out of here."

"How?" Betty and I cried at the same time.

"You can't see what I'm holding in my hand," Wendell whispered. "It's a key."

"A key to the safe?" I asked, my voice high and shrill.

"Turn around," he replied. "Carefully. Turn around and watch."

Betty and I bumped elbows as we slowly spun to the back of the safe.

"Shhh. Don't make a sound," Wendell whispered.

I sucked in another deep breath and held it.

I heard a *click*. The click of the key, I guessed.

Then I saw a slit of dim light. It slowly grew wider as Wendell pushed open the back of the safe.

I blinked, waiting for my eyes to adjust.

Wendell pushed the back all the way open. He held a finger to his lips as he led the way out.

Betty and I stepped out into the basement. Both of us were breathing hard. I felt so happy, I wanted to leap into the air and do a dance.

Wendell tucked the key into his pocket. "You can't say I'm not prepared," he said. He peered around the basement. "No sign of them."

“What are we going to do?” Betty asked.

“We have to get out of the house,” Wendell answered. “Without being seen.” He cupped a hand around his ear and listened hard. “They said they were going to search the house from top to bottom. If we’re lucky, they started at the top. And we can sneak out easily.”

“But where are we going?” I demanded. “Aren’t you going to call the police or someone?”

Wendell raised his finger to his lips again. “Shhh. There are no police out here by the forest, Billy. They are four or five towns away. We’re on our own, I’m afraid.”

“But what are we going to *do*?” my sister repeated.

Wendell narrowed his eyes at both of us and whispered softly, “We have to get that book before they do.”

DON'T MAKE A SOUND!

There really *was* a scariest book ever? It was *real*?

I started to ask Wendell. But he put a finger over my lips. "Don't make a sound," he whispered.

He waved us toward the stairs. Moving slowly, carefully, he slid his shoes on the concrete floor so they wouldn't make any noise.

Betty and I followed close behind him. My legs still trembled from being locked in the safe. And I kept shaking my head, trying to send away my frightening thoughts.

We stopped at the bottom of the stairwell and listened.

Silence.

Wendell nodded and led the way up the stairs. I leaned heavily on the banister so my footsteps would be light.

We stepped into the gray light of the top basement and gazed around. No one here. Betty and I followed him to the stairway that led up to the first floor.

"If they're in the attic or somewhere upstairs, we'll be okay," Wendell whispered. He peered up the stairwell. "We've got to get out of the house. If they catch us, I don't know what they'll do."

"Where are we going?" Betty whispered.

"Into the forest," he replied.

Those words sent a chill down my back.

"I worried a thief might find the book in the house," Wendell whispered. "So I hid it in the forest where no one could ever find it."

"You mean . . ." I started. "The book is real?"

He started up the stairs. "There really is a book," he whispered. "And we have to get it before they do."

"But . . . why did you bring us down to the basement?" Betty asked. "Why did you bring that safe out of the wall?"

Wendell raised his finger to his lips again. "No time for questions. We have to move fast. We have to get out of here before they realize we're gone."

We climbed the stairs and stepped into the back

hallway. Another chill rolled down my back as we stopped to listen. I realized I'd been holding my breath. I let it out in a long whoosh.

Wendell raised his eyes to the ceiling and pointed. "Hear the footsteps? They're both upstairs. If we're totally silent, we can make it to the back door."

We followed Wendell, tiptoeing down the long hall. I heard footsteps and soft thuds above us. The Bookworm and Jesse were probably moving shelves around, searching hard.

The hallway made a sharp turn. I could see the bright light of the kitchen up ahead.

Without saying anything, we began to trot. My heart pounded in my chest. I ignored my rubbery legs and the chill that tightened the back of my neck.

We're going to make it. We're going to make it!

Wendell reached the kitchen and waved us forward. "Hurry!" he whispered. "Not a sound!"

I burst into the kitchen. And opened my mouth. And . . .

"AHHH-CHOOOO!"

DOG TROUBLE

The loudest sneeze of my life?

Wendell and Betty spun around and glared at me in horror.

"S-sorry," I stammered.

I heard a heavy *thud* on the floor above us. Rapid footsteps up there.

"They heard that," Wendell said. "They're coming. Let's go!" He and Betty darted to the kitchen door.

"Oh no!" I couldn't help it. I let out a cry as I crashed into a kitchen chair. It toppled over and clattered loudly onto its side on the floor.

The noises from upstairs grew closer. I knew they *had* to hear that.

Were we going to make it outside?

Wendell pulled on the kitchen doorknob. He tugged it harder. Then he tugged again.

"It—it's stuck!" he cried.

He twisted the knob left and right and pulled. “Always have trouble with this door,” he murmured. His teeth clenched, he jiggled the knob this time, then yanked it hard.

“Oh!” Wendell staggered back as the door finally cracked open. He swung it open wide, and the three of us burst out of the house.

Our shoes pounded the grass. We ran into the night, gray clouds low in the purple sky. A cool wind blew at us from the forest.

Wendell spun around and peered back at the house. “We’re okay!” he cried. “I don’t think they’re coming. Maybe they didn’t hear us.”

He started running again. “We’ll be safe if we can get to the trees.”

Betty and I trotted after him. We didn’t look back. I kept my eyes straight ahead on the shadowy forest in front of us. I didn’t want to see the two thieves coming after us with their flamethrower.

I stopped and almost stumbled when I heard the loud barking.

Betty and I both turned. I saw Bellamy on his hind legs, pulling on his leash. Barking at us. Barking and howling at the top of his lungs.

"Noooo! Quiet, Bellamy!" I shouted. "Be QUIET!"

He gave a powerful pull. The chain snapped. He burst free!

Barking excitedly, Bellamy came racing toward us.

His tail wagged furiously. He leaped onto Betty, barking his excitement. She staggered back, struggled to keep her balance as the dog greeted her so happily.

Then, still barking, he turned to me and jumped at my chest.

"Bellamy—stop!" I cried. "Be quiet! Be quiet!"

I gasped when I saw the kitchen door swing open. The Bookworm leaped out of the house, waving his machete in front of him. He must have grabbed it from the forest path.

The dog didn't care about the Bookworm. He barked and jumped on me happily.

I saw the Bookworm rocketing toward us over the tall grass. I tried to shove the dog away so I could run.

"Bellamy—" I cried. "What have you done?"

30

A LOT OF SLIMY SLITHERING

"Stop! Stop right there!" the Bookworm screamed at us as he ran. "You can't get away!"

I shoved Bellamy with both hands. "Down, boy. Get down."

Betty and Wendell went running to the trees. I tried to run, but Bellamy pawed at my legs. He just didn't get it. He thought it was a game.

"Stop and I won't hurt you!" the Bookworm screamed.

Bellamy suddenly dropped to all fours. The dog turned away from me. He spun toward the screaming man and uttered a long, low growl. Then he lowered his head and took off, racing toward the Bookworm.

"Billy—run!" I heard Wendell shout.

But I had my eyes on Bellamy. Snarling angrily, the big dog leaped onto the Bookworm. Bellamy snapped his jaws at the thief's wrist.

The Bookworm fell backward onto the grass. Barking and growling, Bellamy tore at the sleeve of the man's shirt.

To my surprise, the Bookworm didn't move from the ground. Had he hit his head on something?

I didn't wait to see. I turned, lowered my shoulder like a football running back, and headed for Wendell and my sister.

I could hear Bellamy barking beyond the trees. And then I heard the Bookworm shouting at him. The thief was back in action.

"We have to hide," Wendell said. "We don't want to lead him to the book. Let's hide and wait for him to go past."

He turned in a full circle, his eyes moving over the ground and trees.

Under the tangled tree limbs, it was blacker than night. I hugged myself against the chill of the wind.

"Hey, look," I said, pointing just beyond a clump of weeds. "That mound of dirt over there. We could hide behind it."

"Yes. Let's go," Wendell said. "Hurry. Get behind it. The mound will hide us, and we can watch from there."

We scampered toward the low dirt hill and dropped down on our stomachs behind it.

"Stay low," Wendell whispered. "He won't be able to see us if we keep low."

I heard the crunch of the thief's running footsteps. He was in the forest now, moving between the trees. Close . . . so close.

I lowered myself and tried to dig myself into the dirt.

"Oh, wait," I murmured. "Wait. Oh no. Nooooo."

The mound was moving!

"Not dirt!" Betty squealed. "Whoa. Not dirt!"

I raised myself to my knees. My stomach lurched as I realized what we were lying on top of.

Worms. An enormous sticky mountain of huge, wet worms.

I started to gag as worms slithered over my body, my face. Fat purple worms clung to my arms, my shoulders, and the front of my shirt.

"Stay down. Stay down! He'll see you!" Wendell whispered loudly.

But my skin itched so hard! I had to brush the worms off my face. There were worms slithering down my neck, down the front of my shirt.

Betty was groaning. "Sick. Oh, sick." She pulled two fat worms from her hair and tossed them back on the pile.

I slapped a worm from behind my ear.

"Stay down. The Bookworm is coming!" Wendell cried in a loud whisper. Worms crawled and slithered over him, but he didn't seem bothered by them. He didn't move from the mound.

"I—I can't *stand* it!" my sister shrieked.

She jumped to her feet, slapping worms off her arms, pulling them from her shirt.

"Get down! Betty—get down!" I cried. I grabbed her arm. I tried to tug her back down.

Too late.

Too late.

The Bookworm saw her.

31

CAVE OF THE LOCUST

"Run!" Wendell shouted, struggling to his feet.

I dug my hands into the worm pile and started to push myself up. But my hands slipped out from under me over the slimy worms. And I fell facedown, back into the pile.

Sputtering, spitting out worms, I raised my head and stumbled to my feet. Betty and Wendell were already running through the trees.

I could hear the Bookworm shouting, close behind me.

I lowered my head and picked up speed, trying to catch up to them.

Wendell led the way through the trees to a small clearing. Under the moonlight, tall weeds swayed from side to side in a swirling breeze. Suddenly, loud, raspy birdcalls rose up from the trees, as if the birds were warning us away.

“There it is!” Wendell cried, pointing ahead. “The Cave of the Locust.”

I squinted hard. I could just barely make out a tall mountain of gray stone at the other side of the clearing. And a black cave opening carved into it.

Wendell motioned us forward with his hand and began trotting toward the cave. We jogged fast to keep up with him.

“I hid the book in the cave,” Wendell said. “I knew no one would look for it there.”

We stepped through the cave opening. Wendell pulled a slender halogen flashlight from his back pocket and shone it into the darkness.

“Hey—!” I let out a cry as two manbats came flying toward us. Flapping hard, they swooped near my head. I could see their startled human faces before they soared out of the cave and headed to the trees.

The circle of light danced over the cave walls. The cave appeared empty. I could see a tunnel way at the back.

“Let’s go.” Wendell’s voice echoed off the stone walls. Shining his light ahead of us, he led the way into the darkness.

I shivered. The air in the cave was cold, cold enough

to see my breath. My shoes scraped over the thick carpet of dust on the cave floor.

"This is creepy," Betty whispered. Her words rang in the air.

"*Everything* here is creepy," I said. "If only Mom and Dad knew . . ."

I stopped when I heard a tapping sound up ahead.

Wendell stopped, too. He raised a hand to his ear to listen.

I heard it again. Tapping on the cave floor. A little closer.

Click click click click.

"Uh-oh," Wendell murmured. He took a couple steps back. "I think we have a problem."

"P-problem?" I stammered. "What problem?"

"I think we woke up the cave locust."

LOCUST ATTACK

"The cave locust sleeps for weeks at a time," Wendell whispered. "I was hoping it was still asleep—" Wendell stopped midsentence.

The tapping footsteps grew louder until they sounded like drumbeats on the cave floor. The sounds echoed off the stone walls. So loud, I covered my ears with my hands.

"Noooo." A cry escaped my throat as a giant insect stormed up in front of us. It rose high, towering above us like a creature in a horror movie.

Yelping, Betty and I staggered back from the enormous insect.

It was at least eight feet tall. A stick figure, except its legs were as thick as baseball bats. The front and rear legs tapped up and down as it lowered its head toward us. Its giant head—the size of a soccer ball!

Two snakelike antennae waved on top of the head.

And red eyes the size of oranges appeared to spin as it studied us.

"It—it can't be real!" Betty cried. "No insect is as big as a house!"

Wendell had his eyes locked on the locust's rolling eyes. "It's real," he said. "Without any humans here for hundreds of years, the insects have been allowed to grow wild."

Tapping loudly, it inched closer. Its head lowered as if ready to attack.

We backed up some more. Now we were against the cave wall. Nowhere to move.

The creature's thin wings fluttered on its slender back. The red eyes spun wildly as it continued to study us.

"We're not going to disturb you!" Wendell shouted. "We just came for the book. Let us take the book, and we will leave you in peace."

A long pink tongue curled from the insect's open jaws.

Trembling in fear, I bumped up against Wendell. "Does it speak English?"

"I—I don't think so," he stammered. "But I thought it was worth a try."

The insect moved fast to attack. I opened my mouth to scream. But no sound came out.

Jagged fangs appeared in the creature's open mouth. It let out an angry *hiss.* Then it lowered its head—stuck out its tongue—and licked my face.

"It—it likes me!" I cried.

"No!" Wendell shouted. "Its tongue—the venom—is *poison*!"

33

HUNGRY LOCUST

The locust lowered its head to lick me again.

I stuck my hands up to protect myself, but it was too enormous to shove away. The big insect snapped at me.

Snapped again.

I gazed up at it. What was it *chewing*?

In my panic, I saw the fat purple worm wriggling in its mouth. The insect had swiped a worm from my shirt pocket.

Betty screamed as the creature dipped its head—and pulled a worm from her hair. The antennae on its head stood straight up as it chewed noisily. Its wings fluttered excitedly.

"Oh, wow. It likes the worms," Wendell said. "Do you have more still on you?"

I rubbed my chest and pulled a worm from under my shirt.

"Feed it to him," Wendell said. "Keep feeding him. That will keep him busy. And I'll go grab the book."

He took off, trotting into the darkness at the back of the cave.

Betty ran her hands through her hair. Then she rubbed her T-shirt. "Billy, I—I don't have any more worms," she said in a trembling voice.

My leg itched. I pulled up my jeans cuff and tugged a worm off my thigh. I held it up to the insect. His head dove down and swiped it from my hand.

While he chewed noisily, I searched myself up and down for more.

I pawed my shirt, my pants, my socks. "Oh no. Oh no," I murmured. "All out. I'm all out."

She frantically tore at her hair. "I—I can't find any. What are we going to do?"

The giant insect brought its head down to us, red eyes glowing.

"It's waiting for more," I said. "But—"

It uttered another long *hiss*.

"I think it's getting ready to attack," Betty said.

My eyes darted around the cave. We were backed against the wall. Nowhere to run.

"Wendell! Wendell!" I screamed.

No reply.

"Wendell—help us!"

The fanged jaws moved up and down. The insect turned from Betty to me. The antennae swayed from side to side.

I prepared to duck. Maybe if I hit the floor . . . I could roll out from under it.

I watched the big head stretch up. The jaws snapped some more.

Then I heard a tapping sound from behind the locust. I squinted into the darkness.

And saw another giant locust moving toward us.

The two huge insects stood side by side, bumping their bony bodies, red eyes locked on us.

We're doomed, I thought. *We don't stand a chance.*

My whole body shivered . . .

. . . and a worm dropped off my shoulder.

How did I miss it?

I watched it hit the cave floor in front of the two locusts.

Both creatures dove for it at once.

As I watched in shock, they began batting heads together. Their legs slapped and kicked as they fought for the worm. The two insects rolled on the cave floor, hissing and snapping at each other.

Eyes on the battling locusts, the two of us slid our backs against the cave wall, edging toward the opening. Then we turned and ran.

I could still hear the locusts fighting as we flew out of the cave and kept running. We didn't stop till we reached a group of tall trees at the back of a clearing. Hidden in their shadow, we leaned on a wide trunk and struggled to catch our breath.

"A close one," I choked out.

Betty squinted toward the cave. "Where is Wendell? Why isn't he coming out?"

I heard a shout. Turned. And saw someone running toward us across the clearing.

Not Wendell. It couldn't be Wendell. He hadn't come out of the cave.

A stranger. Running full-speed.

The man was tall and thin. Coppery hair fell from under a green baseball cap. He wore a gray sweatsuit, the hood bouncing on his back.

"Hey— Hey—" he called to us, waving his arms wildly.

Betty and I were too winded to try to run from him.

We spun away from the tree and huddled together as the man ran up to us.

He stopped, breathing hard, his face red, his blue eyes studying us. “There you are!” he cried finally. “I’ve found you.”

Betty and I stared back at him.

“Who are you?” I managed to ask.

He narrowed his eyes at us. “I’m your uncle Wendell.”

PART THREE

34

BETTY'S REAL NAME

"Noooo!" Betty and I both uttered startled cries.

"Our uncle is in the cave," Betty said. "Who are you?"

He tugged off his baseball cap and smoothed back his rust-colored hair. "He's not your uncle. I am."

"But—but—" I sputtered.

"He's a book thief known as 'the Collector,'" the man said. "I thought he was my friend. He has come to my house many times. I thought I could trust him. I told him too many of my secrets. But he turned out to be a thief."

"But . . . we found him locked in the shed," Betty said. "He told us that—"

"The Bookworm arrived and locked him in the shed. Then the Bookworm tied me up in the attic. It took me all this time to escape."

He looked from Betty to me. "I was so worried about you two."

Betty and I exchanged glances. "How do we know we can believe you?" Betty asked.

"Everyone tells us they're Wendell," I added.

"I just captured the Bookworm and his daughter," he replied. "I found them following the trail in the forest. I took them back to the house and tied them up. Then I was frantic to find you. I've been searching—"

He stopped when a shout rang out through the trees. I spun around and saw the blond-haired Wendell running from the cave. He had a canvas bag, swinging from one hand.

"Yes. That's the Collector," the red-haired man said. "Now I need to capture him, too." He slipped behind a wide tree trunk. "Don't let him know I'm here."

Running hard, the other Wendell spotted us and waved. The bag swung wildly at his side.

I turned to Betty. "What should we do? Who can we believe?"

Before she could answer, the blond Wendell caught up to us. "Got it," he said, raising the bag. "Let's get away from here."

"Not so fast," the new Wendell cried, leaping out

from behind the tree. He reached out both hands. "I'll take the book now, Collector."

"Collector?" He pulled back and swung the bag behind him. "I don't know who you mean. And I don't know who you are. I'm the kids' uncle Wendell."

"You can't keep that up, Collector. You can't fool these kids any longer. And I won't let you get away with my book."

"I'm their uncle. They know me. They know I'm their uncle Wendell."

I studied the man holding the bookbag, the man with the blond hair. Then I turned my gaze on the one with red hair falling under his baseball cap.

Which one? Which one?

Suddenly, I knew what to do!

I took a step forward. "Only one of you is telling the truth," I said. "But I know how to tell the real Wendell."

Both men stared at me.

"Tell us Betty's real name," I said.

35

"I'LL DEAL WITH YOU LATER"

The blond man squinted at Betty. "That's easy," he said. "It's Elizabeth."

I crossed my arms in front of me. "You're wrong," I said.

"I saw Betty a few weeks after she was born," the red-haired man said. "Her real first name is Bethany."

"Correct," Betty said.

The blond man—the Collector—uttered a cry and swung the canvas bag at the real Wendell's head. It landed with a *smack* and Wendell staggered backward with a groan.

The Collector rushed forward and swung the heavy bag at Wendell again. The bag smacked the back of Wendell's head, harder this time.

He uttered a painful groan. His legs collapsed, and he dropped to the ground.

Betty and I stared down at him in horror. His eyes were closed. He didn't move.

The Collector grabbed me hard by the shoulder and gave me a shove. "Let's go. I've got to get out of here."

"We—we can't leave my uncle there," I stammered. I tried to pull my shoulder free. But his grip was too tight.

"He'll come around later," he said. "By that time, I'll be long gone." He gave me another shove, onto the dirt path that led between the trees. "Move it, kid."

I started to walk. Out of the corner of my eye, I saw Betty.

She dove at the Collector and made a grab for the bookbag with both hands.

He swung it out of her reach, and she flew forward, falling into the dirt.

"Get up," he said. "Don't try to be a hero, *Bethany.*" He spit out her name as if it was a curse word.

Muttering under her breath, Betty pulled herself to her feet and wiped the knees of her jeans.

"Now that I have the scariest book ever," the Collector said, "my collection is complete. This book will make me a rich man. And a powerful man."

He stepped behind us and gave us both a shove. "Let's go, you two."

We started to walk. Moonlight flashed through the trees, blocked at times by the tree limbs overhead.

"I have a ride coming soon," the Collector said, stepping in front of us to lead the way. "I hope to never see this forest or the house again."

A chill tightened the back of my neck. "But—what do you plan to do with us?" I choked out.

"I'll deal with you later," he growled.

NOTHING TO SNEEZE AT

We followed the path in silence. I had to force my legs forward. My fear made each leg feel like it weighed a thousand pounds.

Betty had her hands balled into tight fists. She clenched her jaw tightly as she walked beside me. She kept her eyes straight ahead and didn't look at me.

I listened for Wendell. I kept hoping he would come running and rescue us from this evil man. But the only sounds I heard were the scraping of our shoes on the path and the whisper of the trees.

"Ow!" A stab of pain made me cry out and grab my ankle.

The Collector spun around. "What's your problem?"

I leaned over. "I stepped in some burrs," I said. "Ow. Let me pull them out."

"No stalling," he said. "Your uncle isn't going to save you."

"No. I'm serious," I said. I carefully tugged the sticky burrs from my ankle, rubbed it, then stood up.

"Move it, you two," he barked. "I don't want to miss my ride." He swung the bookbag from one hand to the other.

What is he going to do to us? I asked myself for the hundredth time. *What will happen when we get back to the house? Will he lock us in the shed? Or back in that safe?*

My fright nearly froze my whole body.

I felt a tingling in my nose. I couldn't hold it in. I opened my mouth wide in a ferocious *sneeze*!

"Huh?" Betty and I both gasped as a big black form fell in front of us.

I stumbled back as a second one landed inches from us, hitting the dirt with a heavy *thud*.

It took me a few seconds to focus my eyes. Tree bears! Two of them!

My sneeze had brought them crashing down.

"Nooooo!" the Collector let out a shriek as one of the huge bears leaped on him. The bookbag fell to the dirt. The bear leaped onto him, sending the terrified man sprawling to the ground.

The second bear dove onto both of them, snarling and clawing, a fierce, noisy wrestling match.

“Hey—!” A cry made me turn around.

Wendell came racing over the path. He didn’t stop when he saw the two bears battling the screaming Collector. He grabbed the bookbag off the ground. Then he turned to us. “You okay?”

We both nodded.

Wendell gave one of the bears a shove. He grabbed the Collector’s hand and pulled him out from under the other bear.

“Let’s go,” he said. “They won’t leave their tree.”

The Collector was scratched and bleeding. He looked dazed as Wendell led him away.

Snarling a farewell, the tree bears stood side by side and watched as we hurried along the path.

A smile spread slowly over Wendell’s face as the house came into view. Tail wagging furiously, Bellamy came running across the lawn to us.

“This was a good day,” Wendell said. “The final score—Good Guys: one, Book Thieves: zero!”

We all laughed as Bellamy leaped into my arms and licked my face till the skin was red.

37

A HARD CHOICE

"Wendell said you two had a very exciting time," Mom said. "I want to hear all about it."

Dad pulled the car onto the highway. "We have a long drive ahead. Plenty of time for you to share everything with us."

Betty and I exchanged glances across the backseat. Did we really want to tell Mom and Dad the danger we had been in?

I didn't think so.

The animal attacks in the forest. The strange creatures. The fake Uncle Wendells. The giant locusts. The tree bears. The scariest book ever written.

Would they even *believe* any of it?

Betty and I had talked about it before Mom and Dad came to pick us up. We decided maybe we had to go slow and tell it to them a little at a time.

That way, maybe they wouldn't be too shocked or horrified.

Dad sped up. Farm fields whirred by outside the car windows.

"Well . . . start telling us everything," he said. "You two are so quiet. Did you actually have a boring time?"

"It wasn't exactly boring," I said. "It—"

"But we want to hear about *your* trip," Betty chimed in. "How was London? Where did you go? What did you see? What was the best part?"

Mom turned to us from the front seat. "I'll tell you the *worst* part," she said. "We missed the two of you *so much*."

"Next time, we're going to bring you with us," Dad said. "We'll have a real family vacation."

"Yaaaay!" Betty and I both uttered a long cheer.

We dropped our suitcases in the entrance hall. We were both happy to be home. No bats flying around with human heads. No strange cries from a nearby forest.

Dad ran out and brought home a bucket of chicken and a bunch of sides. It tasted so awesome. Normal life.

After dinner, Betty and I went upstairs to our rooms

to unpack. I lugged the suitcase to my bed. When I lifted the lid, I found a surprise.

"Betty—!" I shouted. "I think you'd better get in here. Hurry!"

She came into my room, unfolding some sweaters. "What's your problem, Billy?"

"Look," I said. I pointed to the blue canvas bookbag at the top of my suitcase.

"Oh no," she murmured.

I lifted the bag and peeked inside. I saw the heavy black book. And a small white envelope.

"Oh no. Oh no," Betty repeated.

I opened the envelope and read the note inside:

I knew your house was the safest place to hide the book. Keep it safe. Keep it from all eyes. I know you will protect it. Love, Uncle Wendell

I dropped the note to my bed. My hands shook as I picked up the bookbag.

"What shall we do? Where should we hide it?" I asked, my voice trembling.

Betty and I stared at each other, thinking hard.

"I know," Betty said finally. "That storage drawer you never use. At the back of your closet. It's hidden behind all your clothes."

“Yes. Perfect,” I said. I started to the closet. But the bag slipped from my hands—and the book slid onto the bedspread.

Betty and I both reached for it. I lifted it into my arms. It was heavier than I’d imagined. Betty smoothed her hand over the cover.

I set it back down on the bed. Betty and I gazed at each other. I knew we were both thinking the same thing.

I wrapped my fingers around the thick black book cover. “Before we hide it away,” I said, “should we open it? Just one peek?”

ABOUT THE AUTHOR

R.L. Stine says he gets to scare people all over the world. So far, his books have sold more than 400 million copies, making him one of the most popular children's authors in history. The Goosebumps series has more than 150 titles and has inspired a TV series and two motion pictures. R.L. Stine himself is a character in the movies! He has also written the teen series Fear Street, which has been adapted into three Netflix movies, as well as other scary book series. His newest picture book for little kids, illustrated by Marc Brown, is titled *Why Did the Monster Cross the Road?* R.L. Stine lives in New York City with his wife, Jane, a former editor and publisher. You can learn more about him at rlstine.com.

Read on for a creepy sneak peek of *Goblin Monday*!

FIREFLY FREAKS OUT

MomMom suddenly pushed her chair back and climbed to her feet. "Let's all put our spoons down," she said. "Let's sing my favorite winter song. Actually, it's a Christmas song."

Todd leaned close and whispered in my ear. "Uh oh. Here we go. Just do your best. Move your lips and pretend to sing."

MomMom raised her spoon like a conductor's baton. "Everybody sing along," she said.

She cleared her throat loudly and began to sing . . .

The old man is coming,
There's barley in the barn.
The old man will watch you
When you wake up Christmas morn.
The old man will give you a plum.
Give you a plum. He'll give you a plum.
Don't bite it, don't taste it, not on Christmas morn.

She started a second verse, waving her spoon baton. But she stopped after a few words.

Her face turned red again. "Why isn't anyone singing?" she demanded.

"We don't know that song, MomMom," Todd answered.

"*Everyone* knows that song!" she exclaimed.

Something rubbed against my legs. I looked down and saw Firefly, their black cat, staring up at me.

MomMom made a grumpy sound and dropped back in her chair.

Jewel patted her hand. "It's an awesome song, MomMom," she told her. "Will you teach it to me later?"

"You already know it, Jewel. Everyone knows the *Barley in the Barn* song. We sang it in kindergarten."

Grandpa Tweety rolled his eyes. "Let's eat and do our singing after dinner."

"MomMom, you've never given me the recipe for this stew," Mrs. Simms said. I knew she was trying to change the subject. "You really must share it with me."

MomMom shook her head. "I can't. It's a *secret* recipe."

Something caught my eye in the garden. Peering through the glass door, I saw two tall brown rabbits.

They were standing side by side on their hind legs, looking in on us.

I jumped up. "I have to take a picture," I said. I ran up to my room to get my camera.

When I returned, the rabbits were still standing there. I stepped up to the glass doors and started to snap some shots.

But something bumped my legs and nearly knocked me over.

Firefly the cat. The creature let out a long, loud *hiss.*

Firefly attacked the door. Raised himself onto his hind legs. Pounded the glass with both front paws. Shrieking and clawing and scratching, the cat went berserk.

I turned to Grampa Tweety. "What . . . what's wrong with Firefly?" I stammered.

Tweety shrugged. "It's probably the goblin in the garden."

Goosebumps

Read them all—if you dare!

GOOSEBUMPS® HALL OF HORRORS

- ☐ #1 CLAWS!
- ☐ #2 NIGHT OF THE GIANT EVERYTHING
- ☐ #3 SPECIAL EDITION: THE FIVE MASKS OF DR. SCREEM
- ☐ #4 WHY I QUIT ZOMBIE SCHOOL
- ☐ #5 DON'T SCREAM!
- ☐ #6 THE BIRTHDAY PARTY OF NO RETURN!

GOOSEBUMPS® MOST WANTED

- ☐ #1 PLANET OF THE LAWN GNOMES
- ☐ #2 SON OF SLAPPY
- ☐ #3 HOW I MET MY MONSTER
- ☐ #4 FRANKENSTEIN'S DOG
- ☐ #5 DR. MANIAC WILL SEE YOU NOW
- ☐ #6 CREATURE TEACHER: THE FINAL EXAM
- ☐ #7 A NIGHTMARE ON CLOWN STREET
- ☐ #8 NIGHT OF THE PUPPET PEOPLE
- ☐ #9 HERE COMES THE SHAGGEDY
- ☐ #10 THE LIZARD OF OZ
- ☐ SPECIAL EDITION #1 ZOMBIE HALLOWEEN
- ☐ SPECIAL EDITION #2 THE 12 SCREAMS OF CHRISTMAS
- ☐ SPECIAL EDITION #3 TRICK OR TRAP
- ☐ SPECIAL EDITION #4 THE HAUNTER

GOOSEBUMPS® SLAPPYWORLD

- ☐ #1 SLAPPY BIRTHDAY TO YOU
- ☐ #2 ATTACK OF THE JACK!
- ☐ #3 I AM SLAPPY'S EVIL TWIN
- ☐ #4 PLEASE DO NOT FEED THE WEIRDO
- ☐ #5 ESCAPE FROM SHUDDER MANSION
- ☐ #6 THE GHOST OF SLAPPY
- ☐ #7 IT'S ALIVE! IT'S ALIVE!
- ☐ #8 THE DUMMY MEETS THE MUMMY!
- ☐ #9 REVENGE OF THE INVISIBLE BOY
- ☐ #10 DIARY OF A DUMMY
- ☐ #11 THEY CALL ME THE NIGHT HOWLER!
- ☐ #12 MY FRIEND SLAPPY
- ☐ #13 MONSTER BLOOD IS BACK
- ☐ #14 FIFTH-GRADE ZOMBIES
- ☐ #15 JUDY AND THE BEAST
- ☐ #16 SLAPPY IN DREAMLAND
- ☐ #17 HAUNTING WITH THE STARS
- ☐ #18 NIGHT OF THE SQUAWKER
- ☐ #19 FRIIIGHT NIGHT

ALSO AVAILABLE:

- ☐ SPECIAL EDITION: SLAPPY, BEWARE!
- ☐ IT CAME FROM OHIO!: MY LIFE AS A WRITER by R.L. Stine